MIRIAM'S DILEMMA

by
Donna Adee

MIRIAM'S DILEMMA
Copyright © 1997 by Harvest Publications

Printed in the United States of America

Cover art by Ann Gower
Inside Illustrations by Tony Hoffhines

Page design & layout by Good Shepherd Publications,
Hillsboro, Kansas

Library of Congress Catalog Number 97-77669
ISBN 0-9654272-1-8

ACKNOWLEDGMENTS

First, I wish to thank God for giving me the ability to write, and for Erin, our teenage granddaughter and Lindsey, our "adopted granddaughter" who read each chapter and helped me see the story through their eyes.

I wish to thank Ann Gower for her encouragement, her many hours working on the cover, and posing two untrained teenage models in 1895 clothing to authentically represent the dress of girls of that time period.

Also, thanks to Janet Catlin who read each page carefully, checking for spelling and grammatical errors, and to Charity Bucher of Good Shepherd Publications, for guiding me through another book printing.

A special thanks to Ellis, my husband of forty years, who patiently waits for late meals and encourages me to keep on writing.

CHAPTER ONE

THE MOVE TO THE BARREN PLAINS

MIRIAM JENSEN looked wistfully out the window as they left Kansas City on the Missouri Pacific carrying her and her mother and sisters to their new home in Beloit. Her father, Aaron, had seen a poster asking for blacksmiths to locate in the new town of Beloit, Kansas, which was a growing city in 1895. Skills of this type were much needed to keep the farm machinery repaired and the horses shoed. She felt like stopping the train immediately, demanding that it turn around and take them to their home in Kansas City. She had to think of some way to convince her father to let her return to Kansas City for school that fall. She kept mulling over in her mind, "I'm not going to be stuck in a little humdrum town for the whole school year! I'll run away if Father insists I stay."

Her mother, Lydia Jensen, seeing her sadness, whispered in her ear, "I know it hurts to leave, but God may have something magnificent for us in Beloit. I, too, am sorry to leave Kansas City and our friends, but your father has made this choice."

Miriam whimpered, "But he didn't ask if we wanted to leave all our friends and nice house to come to this boring place." Miriam was sad that her beautiful mother looked so tired and unhappy. "Father must have made a mistake asking us to move," she thought.

Aaron had left his flourishing Kansas City business to start his new shop. After two months, he was ready for the family to join him. The simple farm house that he had hired built was almost ready for his wife and five little girls.

Miriam knew that her mother wasn't convinced that Beloit was the place she wanted to raise a family. How could living in a town that had only become a second class city in 1875 compare with life in Kansas City? Miriam knew she and Anna would miss their excellent music teachers and art museums and concerts, but she remembered hearing her parents pray about this move. She appreciated her mother's willingness to go wherever her father chose to live and work even though it was difficult leaving the few family members who were still living. Great-Grandmother Millie had died last year; she had been Lydia's mother since she was ten, after her mother's death. Miriam remembered her mother's story of moving in with Grandma Millie and how they were a family until Grandpa's death when her mother was sixteen. But there were aunts and uncles and cousins living in Kansas City. There would be no one in Beloit who were friends or family. "It will be terrible, miserable, and unbearable. I know I will hate every minute of our move," Miriam fumed.

North Central Kansas sounded hot, dry and barren to

Miriam, who so enjoyed the beautiful trees and hills of Johnson County. Their two-story house surrounded by stately oak trees had been her home since her birth. "I bet Mary and Eliza won't write as they said they would. They think that mail doesn't go that far west. I wish Mother had let me stay and live with Aunt Mable; at least I would have a good school and piano lessons. At thirteen, I can be away from Mother and Father. Maybe if I keep pestering, they will send me back," Miriam consoled herself.

Miriam's sulking came to a sudden halt as the train jerked to a stop. "Where are we?" she asked in panic. "We just passed Topeka so we can't be there yet. There isn't even a town here!" she exclaimed as she glanced out the window.

A conductor walked quickly through the car, "We'll be on our way in a minute, folks. Everything's all right. Just a farmer with a cow stuck on the tracks. Sit tight and we'll be headin' on our way shortly."

"I suppose this is what it will be like in Beloit. Cows in the streets and buffalo running wild and Indians ready to attack any minute! I know I'm going to hate this little one-horse town," Miriam grumbled.

"Don't you remember that Father said that there weren't any buffalo around Beloit and there hadn't been any for several years. He said so many had been killed off that the Indians are having trouble finding enough food," Anna reminded her.

"I still don't like being out in the middle of nowhere. Can't I go back to Kansas City in September and stay with Aunt Mable for the school year, Mother?" Miriam begged.

"Miriam, please don't talk like that. This isn't easy for any of us. Look for something good about the trip. You haven't even noticed the pretty wildflowers in pastures that we passed. You might be in for some surprises," Lydia sighed.

As they neared their destination after a long tiring day of travel, Lydia told Miriam, "I will need your help when we arrive. It will take awhile to set up furniture in our new house and the water will have to be carried from the well. Your father wrote that the men built the outhouse last week so he felt that it was time for us to come."

Miriam looked exasperated. "You mean we have to set up our own furniture? Won't there be some men to help us? Or a water pump in the house? And we will have to use an outhouse? That will be horrible, dreadful and disgusting. How can Father do this to us?"

"Miriam, that is no way to talk about your father. As soon as we get settled, you and Anna will have to help with the washing as it will take all day to scrub the clothes out on the board and rinse them in the tubs," her mother continued. We won't have the help of someone like Mrs. Jones whom we had in Kansas City. I will depend on you to help me start heating the water on the wood cooking stove. I'm so thankful that you girls know how to sew because it will take all my time to do the cooking and start a garden. Your father said that he had found a man to plow the garden with his one-horse plow," Lydia explained patiently.

Anna, a perky, dark haired ten-year-old, said, "What will I be doing, Mother? Won't we be able to go to the park like we did in Kansas City, and play on the swings?"

"I'm afraid that for a few weeks both of you will be too busy to play. Since you know how to bake bread now, Anna, that will be your special job," her mother said.

Jessie, age four, with her long blond hair bouncing asked, "What can I do, Mommy? Will there be any friends for me to play with?"

"I don't think there are many children living in Beloit yet. It's a very small town and they are advertising for families to move to this rich farming community. It won't be like Kansas City," Lydia replied.

"There probably aren't any children in Beloit," Miriam pouted. "People don't go to far away places like Beloit to live."

"That is enough, Miriam! If you can't say something nice, I want you to keep your thoughts to yourself," Lydia scolded.

Emma, age two, with long blond hair, whimpered. "I want Papa. I'm so hungry!"

"We've packed some jerky, some of Anna's cookies and dried fruit for our trip, but we will have to find neighbors who have a cow and chickens for our eggs and milk. Your father may know of someone nearby. How would you like to help make the butter, Emma? You could crank the butter churn so we will have butter for the bread that Anna will be making," Lydia answered.

Tabitha, age fifteen months, started to cry and Lydia lifted her from Miriam's arms, "Don't cry little one; we will soon be in our new home. Your bed is small so we can set that up for you to sleep as soon as we arrive. Daddy said that he has a man building closets. We may have to sleep on the floor for a few days on our straw ticks (mattresses stuffed with straw) if we can't find some men to help set up the beds."

At last the train squealed to a stop in Beloit. The

horse-drawn wagons stirred up dust from the streets as they drove by. Miriam complained, "Where is Papa? I thought he would be here to meet us."

"Could that black-covered man over there be your father? It sure looks like him. I didn't realize this blacksmithing would get him so dirty. I hardly recognized him," Lydia chuckled.

Aaron drove up with a horse-drawn wagon. "Get in, girls. I'll get your trunks and deliver you to our new house. I have some men over there ready to unload the furniture and they will help set it up. I must hurry back to work."

As they drove through town, Miriam exclaimed, "Look at that big New York Mercantile Company! That's bigger than some in Kansas City."

"There is the First National Bank and on the other side the Beloit State Bank. There's Jonte and Company, grocery store, next door. You didn't tell me about all these shopping places, Aaron!" Lydia exclaimed.

"I was too busy to spend much time checking out shopping. Remember, I came here to start a business and build a house. Don't you think I did quite well in two months?" Aaron asked with a crooked smile.

Lydia laughed. "Yes, I trust you to take care of us, but it would have been more appealing for the girls and me to know that there are so many stores. Is that a newspaper office?"

"Yes, there are five newspapers in town. *The Beloit Gazette* office is over there. They advertise subscriptions to the *Gazette* and *New York Tribune* or *The K.C. Star* for $1.50 a year. On that side street is the *Beloit Weekly Courier* with the feisty W.H. Caldwell as editor. He adds editorial color to the news."

"What about doctors and dentists? Do they have any?" Lydia asked.

Aaron nodded, "Well, if you notice, over there is Dr. F.M. Daily's office near the New York store. Dr. S. O'Brian, physician and surgeon, has an office over the Hart Bank building. There are several dentists. but the one I noticed, because of her advertisement as being the only woman dentist in Beloit, is Ora B. Shively. She advertises satisfaction and all work warranted, or money refunded; also magnetic tooth extraction. I don't know any more than that."

"Papa, is there somewhere we can get candy?" Jessie asked, pulling on her father's sleeve.

"Oh, yes, I saw many jars of candy at the Emmert Drug Store. Probably the Bunch-Miller Drug store has candy also. They even sell paint and wallpaper."

"Where can I purchase sewing supplies for our dresses? I hope I don't have to have fabric sent from Kansas City. I want to check the quality myself," Lydia pondered.

"I saw an advertisement in the Gazette for a James Harper store carrying all those kinds of sewing materials you talk about. Silks, laces, dimities, and organdies are some I can remember. Sounds like they would have a big assortment," Aaron answered.

Once in the yard of their farm home on the outskirts of town, Lydia exclaimed, "They do have trees here! Look at the huge oak tree in our yard! You didn't tell me anything about there being trees. Everyone told me it was treeless out here."

Aaron laughed, "You didn't ask about trees. I was needing lumber and found that at Mr. Hersey's saw mill.

We are near the Solomon River so the trees grow tall here. Our neighbors, the Smiths, have a large orchard which produces very well. Althea told me they expect a huge apple crop this year. I'm sure she will sell us some for winter."

Lydia shook her head in surprise. "This isn't what I expected at all. What other surprises can you tell me about?"

"Well, you will have to wait until I come home this evening. I have work waiting for me as soon as I get your trunks in the house," Aaron said, hurrying the baggage inside.

"Doesn't look like much to me," Miriam muttered under her breath. She carried Tabitha into the house and came back for more luggage.

Later, as the girls surveyed their new home, Miriam said, "This doesn't seem like a very exciting place to live. Bet nothing happens here. I miss my friends already. We were soon to get telephones in Kansas City. I'll bet they don't even have a theater here!"

"You may be in for some amazing developments. There have already been surprises," Lydia chuckled.

Miriam, still sulking about the loss of friends and the thought of being stuck in this boring place, slowly helped her mother sort out some cookware and bedding for their first evening in their new house. "Mother, can Anna and I go for a walk and get out of this stuffy house?"

"Of course, Miriam, if you will take Jessie and Emma so I can find something for our evening meal. They have been cooped up on that train for so long, they are driving me crazy with their running in the house," Lydia responded wearily.

"Come on you two. Let's go check out our farm.

Maybe we will see some wild animals or Indians, anything to make this place more exciting," Miriam called to the girls.

"Wild animals! I'm not going out there if there are wild animals," Emma cried.

"Miriam, quit trying to scare her. There aren't any wild animals this close to town. Now take the girls and go for a nice long walk. Father will be coming before long and I need to have something prepared to eat," Lydia demanded.

The girls walked all around the yard looking at the wildflowers and the horses in the neighbor's pasture. Emma kept pointing at all the wildflowers saying, "Look at this little purple one, see that yellow one, can I pick this pink one?" Soon she had her chubby hands full of flowers.

Miriam said, "See the mulberry tree over there, let's go see if the mulberries are ripe. We had those in Kansas City. The little girls ran ahead and as they ran through some tall weeds and wild sunflowers, they came upon a little fox eating mulberries. Jessie came running back screaming, "There's a wild animal in here! He's going to eat us!"

Miriam couldn't see any animal, but Anna, who was closer, saw the fox run away. "I don't think he's going to eat you. With all your screaming, he is the one who is scared," she laughed.

The mulberries were ripe, so the girls picked handfuls and ate until they were purple to their elbows. Miriam looked horrified, "What is Mother going to say? The last time we ate mulberries she couldn't get the stains out of our dresses. Let's go home now and see if we can wash at the well before she sees how bad we look. Emma, your whole face is purple."

The girls washed at the well while Miriam pumped the water. "It's no use," Anna moaned. "What will Mother say when she sees our dresses? We have to tell her right away so she can work on the stains before they set. Maybe if we tell her we will pick mulberries for her to make a pie, she will forgive us."

Lydia was shocked to find her daughters had turned purple. Instead of scolding them, Lydia started laughing. "You girls should see yourselves. Father will die laughing at his purple girls. Now, do you still think Beloit will be so boring?"

"We haven't told you about the fox that scared Emma and Jessie when they surprised him eating mulberries. They were sure he would eat them," Miriam laughed.

At supper that night the girls told their father all of their adventures. He had already guessed what they had eaten. After supper the family thanked God for their safe arrival. Each of the girls prayed before Father prayed. Emma said, "Thank You, Jesus for those yummy berries."

"Thank You, Lord, for making our day exciting," was Miriam's surprising prayer. She knew her father expected her to pray even though she really didn't feel like it. It had been fun but she wouldn't admit she enjoyed her first day.

Lydia glanced up at her in surprise before she prayed, "Thank You, Lord, for showing Miriam that You do care about her homesickness."

Father's prayer expressed the thankfulness of having his family with him at last, "Thank You, God, for Your love and care and the safe arrival of my wonderful family."

It didn't take long for most of the family to fall asleep that night, even though they had to sleep on the floor. But

Miriam lay on her straw mattress pouting, "I still don't like this miserable place. Why did You make us come out here, God? Don't You care if we have friends and a nice house? I know I am going to hate this desolate town." With tears sliding out from under her eyelids, she finally fell asleep.

CHAPTER TWO

THE NEW HOME

EARLY THE NEXT MORNING, all of the girls, except baby Tabitha, were up ready to explore their new location. "Hurry, Miriam!" called Anna as she brushed her long dark hair. "Mom says that we can walk through town before we start helping her unpack."

Miriam's eyes were still red from her tears over night. She muttered to herself, "Bet there isn't anything interesting to see."

Jessie pleaded, "Can't I come too? I want to meet some children my size to play with."

"No, you must stay here and play with Emma." Lydia answered. "You know that she won't play by herself and I must find where I packed our flour and other staples so I can cook breakfast."

Miriam tied her light brown hair into a bun at the back of her neck and pulled on her pink calico dress. In a grumpy tone, she called, "I'll be right out, Anna. I'm having trouble finding my hair combs. If we were back in Kansas City, my clothes and hair bows would be in a dresser not stuffed in trunks."

Her mom looked up sharply from her unpacking. "What was that you said, Miriam? With that kind of attitude, I shouldn't allow you to leave. I will expect a better attitude when you return. Understand?"

"Yes, Mother. I just hate this boring place and I can't pretend I like it, 'cause I don't. In Kansas City, we could go to the library or to the children's theater programs. There probably aren't any girls my age in town, and if there are, they probably don't know anything about music or art," Miriam complained as she stomped out the door.

Soon the girls were walking along the dirt street in front of their house. Beside their house was a farm with cows, sheep and several large work horses. They could see a lady in a bonnet hoeing the garden. She called to them as they walked by, "Hello girls, you must be our new neighbors. I asked your father if he had a family. I'm glad to have company. There aren't very many families in our part of town yet. My name is Althea Smith and my children are all grown and married. Tell your mother that any time she needs eggs or milk, we have plenty to sell."

Miriam put on her best manners and smiled, "Oh, thank you, Mrs. Smith. Mother said that we must find someone who has eggs and milk. I will tell her when we return from our walk."

Althea Smith remarked, "Be sure to check out the livery stable. That is where the action is in this town."

"Where is the livery stable?" asked Anna. "We had horses in Kansas City and Father kept them somewhere but he never showed us."

Mrs. Smith pointed west. "It's right at the end of the street. You can't miss it. You will find the grocery-hardware store located next door. You might find that interesting. Your father's blacksmithy is just north of that. Have you been to his shop yet?"

"No. He didn't have time to take us yesterday, and he left before we were out of bed this morning," Miriam answered.

Anna inquired, "Does that hardware store have candy? We should take something back to Jessie and Emma who stayed home with Momma."

"Yes, they have lemon drops and horehound and probably some peppermint. I'm sure they will like that," Mrs. Smith smiled.

Nearing the livery stable, the girls were surprised by a team of black horses pulling a light carriage which came racing along beside them. Anna jumped into the ditch as the carriage came so near it almost knocked her down. "Why can't they watch where they are going?" she exclaimed angrily.

"The driver didn't look like he saw us. Well, they didn't step on you. Let's go see what the hurry was all about," Miriam responded excitedly.

At the livery stable, a bearded man in a black suit jumped down from the carriage and helped a beautiful young girl down. He strutted into the livery stable and demanded, "Have someone take care of my team immediately. I have one horse who needs a shoe. I will be back in an hour for my team."

Miriam whispered to Anna, "I wonder who that is. He sure makes everyone jump. Look at the way those guys run to take care of his horses."

One of the men said, "The editor sure demands a lot

of everyone. We were working on this farm team. They need their horses just as much as Editor Cramton."

"Better get Cramton's horse done first. He pays well even when he demands immediate attention. That daughter of his must have some special party she has to attend. Melody makes her father jump when she snaps her fingers. He spoils her rotten. She never has to wash a dish or hang out the wash. My daughters can't stand her."

Miriam and Anna walked on hoping for another chance to see this Melody Cramton. "Maybe she isn't as spoiled as he says. We didn't have to do the dishes much in our Kansas City home. Wonder where she lives. I haven't seen any homes that look very fancy," Anna mentioned.

At the grocery-hardware they found barrels of pickles, and baskets of potatoes and onions. The candles and kerosene lamps filled one side, while the bolts of dress goods were on the shelf behind the shoes. In some large jars, they found the lemon drops, peppermint and horehound. "I'll take two pieces of peppermint," Miriam told Mr. Duggan, the store keeper. As he looked at them over his spectacles, he stated grumpily, "That will be 2 cents."

"He sure isn't very friendly," Anna commented once they were outside.

On the way home, they met the black team with Mr. Cramton and Melody rushing east past their home. "Let's follow them to see where they live. Maybe we can meet Melody," Miriam suggested. They had to run to keep the team in sight. Suddenly, the team turned into a long drive with a sign at the entrance that read, "Private Property —stay out."

"Well, aren't they snooty! How do they expect company with a sign like that?" Anna exclaimed.

Walking back home, Miriam was deep in thought. "If a girl like Melody lives here in Beloit, maybe it isn't so boring. But how do I meet this protected Melody?"

Once back home, the girls told their mother all the adventures of the morning. "Mom, you should see that Melody Cramton, the editor's daughter."

Lydia, their mother, said "Right now I need some daughters who know how to unpack trunks. While you were gone, the carpenters brought our kitchen cabinets so you can empty these boxes. It would be nice to have these staples where I can find them. After breakfast you girls need to find some eggs and milk. We can store the milk in the well to keep it cool once you find a farmer to sell us some.

Anna said, "We did find Mrs. Smith who will sell us eggs and milk any time and she is right next door."

Once the girls had the food all unpacked, it was time for lunch. Mother had met Mrs. Smith and purchased eggs and milk. "Here, Miriam, you scramble some eggs for our lunch. Your father will be here soon."

"Why can't Anna do the eggs? She knows how to do them better than I do," Miriam grumbled.

"Miriam, do you remember what I told you this morning? I expect a better response from you. Do you understand?"

"Yes, Mother." Grudgingly she threw the eggs into a bowl and beat them as if she were killing snakes. "It's unfair, unjust and unreasonable to make me do all the work just because I'm the oldest," Miriam muttered under her breath.

The afternoon was spent sorting out their clothes and

hanging them in the closets. Emma and Jessie grew tired of helping. "Can't we go somewhere and play on the swings?" Jessie begged.

"There is no park with swings, Jessie. Maybe Father can hang a rope swing in that big tree so we will have our own swing. I didn't see any children your age on our walk but maybe there aren't any in town. Wouldn't surprise me any," Miriam explained with a condescending tone. Under her breath she muttered, "Little sisters can be such a pain at times."

That evening as they sat down at the newly-made table, Mr. Jensen said, "It is so good to have my family with me. It was lonesome here for two months. Would one of you girls find the family Bible so we can read and pray together tonight? I want to thank God for your safe arrival."

Miriam found the Bible for her father but really didn't wish to hear him read. Her mind kept wandering as she thought through plans on how she could meet Melody.

"Miriam, according to John 3:17, why did Jesus come into the world?" Father asked. Miriam, startled, stammered, "I, I, suppose 'cause He wanted to."

Anna started to laugh but covered her mouth at Father's stern look. "Weren't you listening, Miriam?"

"No, Father, I was thinking about Melody," she answered truthfully. She had learned long ago to always tell Father the truth.

Well, since you can only think of Melody, why don't you tell us all about this Melody. Who is she and why does she interrupt our reading of the Scripture?" Father demanded.

"We saw her in a carriage at the livery stable. Surely you have seen Editor Cramton in town. The men at the livery stable said that he demands immediate attention to his needs while other people have to wait. We saw him today with the young girl. Their carriage almost ran into Anna. We followed them home to see...."

"You what?" Father interrupted. "Don't you know it is not ladylike to follow people or to go to their homes without an invitation? Didn't you learn that in Kansas City? Just because you are in a small town doesn't mean you don't mind your manners. Do you understand?"

"Yes, Father. It's just that I hate this boring, annoying and uninteresting place and I thought maybe Melody might know something to do," Miriam pleaded sorrowfully.

"Miriam, I do not want to hear you say that you hate this place again. You have only been here two days and you say you are bored. Have you considered that your mother is worn out and needs your help? I expect you to be up at six in the morning to prepare my breakfast. Now to bed with all of you as soon as we pray."

As they snuggled down to sleep on their straw ticks, Anna whispered to Miriam, "You sure made Father angry. He may never allow us to meet Melody Cramton."

Miriam thought to herself, "I'll find some way to meet her. And Father won't know about it. He doesn't know how lonesome, friendless, and forlorn I am. Not even Mother understands, and she's a woman. Dear God, help me find a way to meet Melody. She looks like an exciting kind of girl." With that prayer, she dropped off to sleep. She was sure Melody would be her kind of friend and that God would answer her prayer soon.

CHAPTER THREE

MEETING MELODY

JESSIE SHOOK MIRIAM AWAKE. "Miriam, wake up! There's a funny sounding bird outside that is saying, 'bob white, bob white!' What is it? Come help me find it."

Miriam rubbed her eyes and tried to concentrate on Jessie's excited chatter. "You heard what? A bird saying, 'bob white, bob white?' I don't believe it."

"Come outside and you will hear it, too!" Jessie exclaimed excitedly while pulling on Miriam's arm.

"Where's Mother? Why didn't you ask her?" Miriam insisted while pulling on her work dress. "Come on, Anna, hurry and get dressed to see this bird that says, 'bob white, bob white.'"

Anna, still half asleep, answered, "Let me sleep, I was having such a nice dream."

"You can't sleep. Remember, Mother said that we had to help with the washing today. Now come on."

Pulling on Miriam's hand, Jessie kept insisting, "Hurry before birdie leaves. Mother is making so much noise pumping water for the washing, she will scare him away."

Miriam knew that Mother had let them sleep and that she needed them to gather wood for the cookstove, to carry in water from the well, and to help with the washing and planting the garden. Hurrying out to her mother, she exclaimed, "Why did you let us sleep so late? Father told us to help you with this work."

"I know, Miriam, but you were sleeping so sound and only Jessie was up so I thought I could have the water pumped. Can you help me carry it to the house to start heating it?"

"No, no, Miriam has to go help me find the bob white birdie." Jessie begged.

"What are you talking about Jessie?" Mother looked puzzled at Miriam. "Do you know what she is talking about?"

"No, but may I go with her for a minute to see if we can find this bird?" Miriam asked.

"She won't be content until you go, so take her to look for her birdie," Mother laughed.

"Walk on tiptoes so you won't scare birdie," Jessie whispered as she tip-toed with very tiny steps. "Listen, there he is again. Did you hear him?"

"Yes, it does make a sound like 'bob-white' but I don't know what kind of bird that is," Miriam replied. "Stand very still so we can tell where he is hiding."

"There it is again, over by that tree. Let's tip-toe over there to see what he looks like," Jessie insisted.

"Look, there are several little brown and gray birds running through the leaves but I don't know what they are," Miriam said. "Oh! There is Mrs. Smith in the garden. Let's go ask her."

Jessie ran to Mrs. Smith's fence and called. "Mrs. Smith what kind of birdie goes, 'bob-white, bob-white?'"

Laughing at Jessie's imitation of the birds, Mrs. Smith said. "That is the sound of the beautiful little quail birds. They run along the ground with their heads back, or if you scare them, they will fly for a short distance. They are good to eat also, but it takes a good many of them to make a meal."

"Thank you, Mrs. Smith for telling Jessie about the birds. She has pestered me all morning to find that little bird. Now, we must hurry back to help Mother with the washing."

"We can't eat my little bob-white birdies. They are so cute," Jessie cried.

"I'm sure we won't be eating your little quail birdies as long as we have other food, so don't worry about them. So stop your crying." Miriam scolded.

By the time they had the water heating, Emma and Tabitha were in the kitchen with Anna, who had the table set for breakfast.

"Thank you, Anna, for starting breakfast. That helps so much on this busy washing day," Mother praised.

By noon, they finally had the washing hung on the lines that Father had built for them.

"My back is killing me," Anna complained, "I don't like standing over that tub all morning rinsing clothes."

While resting from a busy morning, Miriam told Anna, "Wish we had time to check out Melody Cramton's place. Maybe we could find a way to meet her."

Anna, taking a cold sip of milk from the well cooler, responded, "Do you really think we should be snooping around their farm? Father wouldn't like it if he knew about it. Maybe there is a better way to learn about Melody."

"We wouldn't have to tell Father. We could ask Mother to go for a walk and just happen to end up on that road. After all, we don't know the town yet," Miriam suggested.

They weren't long in finding out more about Melody. Althea Smith came to visit that afternoon. She was visiting with Lydia while Miriam and Anna baked cookies, "I do wish that the Cramtons would be more friendly. It seems like once Mr. Cramton became the editor of the *Beloit Gazette* they disappeared behind their hedge tree farm and refused to visit with the townspeople. That might work in a big city, but in this little town it is mighty strange."

Anna and Miriam looked at each other and smiled. They weren't the only ones who thought the Cramtons were strange. Anna asked, "Mrs. Smith, do you know how old Meoldy Cramton is? They were saying at the livery stable that she had lots of parties, but who goes to her parties if they don't visit with anyone?"

Mrs. Smith answered. "From what I hear, there is only one other family in town that has been invited to their parties. Most of their company comes from other towns. People have seen carriages come with strangers driving into the Cramton's lane. They are mighty strange people, if I do say so."

Lydia asked, "How long have the Cramton's lived in Beloit?"

Althea hesitated, "Well, that is a hard question. Mr. Cramton came three years ago and was so friendly and such a good leader helping bring in businesses, that the men elected him mayor. He seemed to be building a house behind that hedge-tree row. It took over a year to build, according to one of the carpenters. More like a mansion, than a house like the rest of us have. His wife and daughter arrived with wagonloads of furniture soon after that. Mr. Cramton stopped helping in town. He only came to the business meetings after his wife arrived. He changed over night.

Lydia, thinking out loud, said, "I wonder if anyone has tried to visit with Mrs. Cramton? She must be lonely."

Althea responded, "Oh, yes, several of us women took cakes and some fresh produce to them, but the maid would open the door, take the food with a 'thank you' and close the door. No one ever was invited in."

Miriam looked at Anna with a gleam in her eye. She beckoned for Anna to come outside with her. "Why don't we take some of these cookies to Melody, and when the maid opens the door say, 'We are to deliver these cookies to Melody in person.' That way she will either have to tell us to go away, or bring Melody. Put on your blue flowered calico and those blue ribbons. I'll change to my white eyelet so we will look our best."

"But what will we tell Mother? Do you really think she will let us go, after what Mrs. Smith said?" Anna questioned.

Miriam answered, "Let me do the talking. I think I can convince her that we have a social call to make. She wants us to learn to be proper young ladies, so she can't disagree."

"I'm not so sure that will convince her. But I will take off this dirty dress and tie my prettiest ribbons in my hair," Anna agreed.

Lydia was so pleased with Miriam's and Anna's help that morning that she consented. "Be sure to be home by 5:30 so your father can have his supper on time," she reminded them.

Jessie saw Anna and Miriam putting on their best dresses. "Let me go, too. You always go places and leave me home," she begged.

Miriam whispered to Jessie, "We will bring you a surprise if you will stay and play with Emma." Jessie didn't say another word. Miriam wasn't sure what the surprise would be, but she had promised.

It was almost a mile walk to the Cramton's lane. They ignored the sign and walked right to the front door. Miriam pulled the knocker. The door opened. There stood Melody herself. For a moment, no one spoke. Anna blurted out, "We made these cookies for you 'cause we wanted to meet you."

Melody looked surprised. "You made cookies for me? No one has ever made cookies just for me before. Won't you come in? I'm here all alone. Mother is away visiting, and it is the maid's day off."

Miriam and Anna couldn't stop looking at the beautiful house. The beautiful pictures and carpets were much like those in homes they had seen in Kansas City. Miriam asked, "Don't you get lonesome with no one but your mother and father?"

"Oh, yes. That is why Mother and Father have all those parties for me, but parties don't make friends. They all go home and I don't see them again until the next party," Melody sighed.

Anna asked, "Would you like to come visit at our

house? You are welcome any time." Miriam poked her in the ribs and frowned. She didn't think Melody would want to come to their little house with the handmade furniture.

Miriam suggested, "We could come visit you anytime you would like to have us, after we finish our chores. You see, there are seven in our family so we help our mother as much as possible."

"Could I come visit you? I get so bored in this big house. There is nothing to do all day. Come, I will pour you some lemonade and we will try your cookies."

After finishing all the cookies, Melody said, "Those were so scrumptious, much better than our cook makes. Would you teach me how to make them?"

Miriam and Anna looked at the grandfather clock with alarm. "Oh no! We were to be home by 5:30 to help Mother with supper. We must run. We will come tomorrow afternoon, if you want us to visit."

Melody suddenly looked scared. "No! You can't then. I-I-will try to come see you. Tell me where you live."

They gave her directions and she let them out. Running down the lane, Miriam said, "Now, why wouldn't she let us come tomorrow? She enjoyed us being there today."

Anna, running ahead, said "Maybe her wicked mother will be home and keep her a prisoner."

As they were running home, Anna reminded Miriam, "You told Jessie you would bring her a surprise. There are some pretty wild daisies. Would that work for a surprise?"

"She loves flowers. That will satisfy her for now," Miriam gasped, as she stopped to catch her breath and pick a handful of flowers.

That night after supper, Father asked, "Is there anything you would like to pray about?"

Anna asked, "Could we pray for Melody Cramton? Something is bothering her. She seems so lonesome and scared."

"How did you learn all this about Melody? Didn't I tell you that a lady doesn't pester people for a visit?"

"Yes, Father, but Mother gave us permission to take her some cookies. We just planned to leave them with the maid, but Melody herself came to the door and invited us in. She was all alone while her mother was visiting," Miriam answered.

"Well, since she invited you in, that is all right, but I don't want you going there until she sends you an invitation. She knows that you are here, so she should contact you. Do you understand?"

"Yes, Father. But what if she wants to come over here?" Anna questioned.

"We'll cross that bridge when we come to it. From all I have heard, the Cramton's don't visit people like us. Their friends come from other towns. So we won't have to worry about them visiting our humble little home."

Miriam didn't say anymore. She knew that there was no use arguing with her father. She muttered to herself as she dressed for bed, "Father never seems to understand that girls need other girls. He wants us to be bored in this dull, humdrum, and monotonous place. If he insists that I can't see Melody, I'm going to pester him to go live with Aunt Mable this fall."

Both girls lay there wondering why Melody was scared to have them visit. Something must be terribly wrong. Anna whispered, "Do you think that Father will complain if Melody comes over?"

"He can't stop her from coming — especially if she comes while he is at work," Miriam grumbled.

CHAPTER FOUR

BAKING DAY
AND THE STORM

EARLY THE NEXT MORNING, Lydia woke Miriam and Anna. "Time to rise girls, we need to bake bread while it is still cool."

As they dressed, Anna said, "I sure wish you would do the bread, Miriam, you are so much better at it. This will only be my second time."

"I helped you last night by peeling the potatoes and helping you start the batter. Grandma's recipe always works well when we use potatoes with the yeast and let it stand overnight. All you have to do now is add more flour and kneed it until you have it stiff enough to shape. Just put it in the pans and after you have the fire stirred up for a good hot oven, bake it for an hour."

Anna said, "But please help me shape the loaves. I always make them so lumpy — not smooth and shiny like you do."

Jessie and Emma were playing outside while Miriam

and Anna were working on the bread. Lydia was planting more tomatoes from the seeds she had started in the house. It was nearing noon; the house was hot, but the bread was almost finished. Miriam said, "Can you finish cleaning up the flour from the table and bowls while I help Mother in the garden? I need to cool off from this hot house. This is one hot day, and with this stove I feel like I've been cooked too."

After a lunch of fresh homemade bread, and butter cooled in the well, Emma and Tabitha were put down for naps. Jessie was making mud pies outside under the trees. Miriam and Anna were reading when Jessie came running to the door exclaiming, "Someone's coming here with horses. She has a beee-utiful dress!"

Anna and Miriam looked at each other. "Could that be Melody? I didn't think she would come. And look at our dresses. Mine has dirt from the garden and yours has flour all over the front. We look a mess," Miriam moaned.

Lydia had already gone outside to see why Jessie was so excited. She, too, was surprised to see a fancy carriage with a beautiful young lady stopping at their house. Miriam and Anna, coming out behind Lydia, whispered, "Mother, this is Melody. Can we serve her some home-made bread on our best dishes?"

Lydia nodded permission while greeting their visitor, "Welcome, Miss Cramton."

Melody waited for the driver to help her down from the carriage. She said to him, "You may come back after me in an hour, Jackson." Holding her long ruffled skirt off the ground, Melody turned her back on the carriage and started towards the house.

Miriam and Anna both spoke at once, "Melody, we didn't think you would come!" Miriam finished, "we have been working all morning, as you can see by our dresses, but do come in out of the hot sun."

"I had to do a lot of talking to convince Mother that I had some visiting to do. And when I told Jackson that I was stopping here, he kept telling me that my mother would not approve. They all seem to know exactly what I should do. They never ask me what I want to do. I just had to get out of the house," Melody complained.

"Melody, anytime you wish to come, you are welcome in our home but always ask permission of your mother. We don't want her worrying about you," Lydia announced.

"She worries even when she knows were I am. Since my little sister died, she is afraid that something will happen to me. Oh! Let's not talk about it. Hm-m-m, what smells so good in here? It smells like homemade bread," Melody said.

"Would you like a slice of bread with fresh made butter?" Anna asked, "I just finished baking four loaves. It was only my third time. I can almost do it without Miriam's help now."

"You do the baking? Our cook does all of our baking. My mother doesn't even know how to bake homemade bread. Would you show me how sometime? Let me know the next time you are going to bake. I want to watch every step so I can do it myself, if you will help me," Melody begged.

"We would be happy to show you, but you would have to stay all morning to see the results. Do you think that your mother would allow you to be gone that long?" Miriam answered.

Melody thought a moment, "No, I suppose she wouldn't, but maybe I can think of some way to get out of the house without her knowing it."

"No, Melody. I will not allow you to come without telling your mother. Do you think it would help if I would talk to your mother?" Lydia responded strongly.

"Oh no! You must not visit my mother. She would never understand. No, you must not come to our house. I will think of some other way," Melody blurted.

Melody was so upset that her hands were shaking as she held the glass of milk and ate her slice of bread. She didn't say anything for a few minutes. Finally she said, "I'm sorry for getting so upset."

"Melody, if you don't want me to visit you mother, I won't. There must be some way that you could visit with her permission. What if I sent your mother a note inviting you to a bread baking party at our house? Would that work?"

Melody didn't answer for a minute. "It might. Mother says invitations to parties are very important. Could you write one for me to take with me? Set the date on your next baking day." At last Melody relaxed. "Could you show me around your house? It looks so interesting."

They were having an enjoyable visit when Aaron burst into the door, "You must all come outside and lie in the gully. A horse and rider came galloping up to the shop just now saying, 'There's a tornado headed this way.'" He rushed out the door to warn the neighbors. Melody began to cry, "I'm scared. I've never seen a tornado." Lydia gathered her into her arms. "Miriam, pick up Tabitha from her bed. Anna, grab Jessie and Emma and follow me." With

Melody clinging tightly, Lydia ran from the cabin to the nearest gully behind the house. Miriam and Anna were right behind her.

"Where's Father?" cried Jessie. "I want Father here."

Lydia assured her with, "Father is warning others so they can go to safer places. God will take care of him. Come, let's all lie down here."

The sky became very dark. The wind almost stood still as the tornado cloud came closer. The little girls began to cry as the wind switched direction and dust began to blow. Miriam held Tabitha tightly as they heard the roar as loud as many freight trains come closer. They could hear trees crashing, and see chunks of wood flying through the air as the tornado roared through. Lydia prayed, "Lord, take care of Aaron and the others in town. This is the place that You led us to live, so we ask Your protection."

Suddenly, it began to rain. Large heavy drops at first, and then a downpour. The wind seemed to be less threatening, so Lydia said, "Let's run for the house. I think the tornado has left." As they ran, she kept praying, "Lord, let there be a house to run to for protection from the rain."

As they neared the house, Miriam sobbed, "Mom, that big tree where our swing hung has been blown down and the outhouse is gone! This is a terrible storm."

"Thank You, Lord, for saving our house," Lydia prayed out loud. Melody looked at her in surprise. She had never heard anyone pray outside of a church building.

"Light the lamps, girls. It is so dark in here," Lydia requested once they were inside. They were soaked and muddy, but safe. "What will your mother think, Melody, when you come home like this? Should we walk you home?"

35

Melody was still shaken up from all the excitement. "I don't know what to do. I suppose Jackson will come for me or maybe he already came and left. Would you walk me to my lane? I can find my way from there."

"Miriam and Anna, you stay here with the little girls and start supper. I will walk Melody home. Tell your father where I have gone."

It was still raining lightly, so Lydia found their umbrella and held it over Melody as they started out. Melody was full of questions as they walked, holding each other tightly under the umbrella. "Mrs. Jensen, you prayed to God right there in the yard when you saw the house was safe. You talk to Him like you know Him. I have never heard anyone pray except in a church, and we haven't had a church to go to since we left St. Louis."

"Melody, I do know Him. In the Bible it tells us that as many as receive Him become the children of God. I did that when I was your age. I am a child of God and you can be also. We can talk to Him anytime, anywhere. Would you like for me to tell you more?"

"Oh, No! Mother wouldn't let me join any other church. I could never be a child of God."

"I'm not talking about joining a church. I would be happy to show you from the Bible more about being a child of God. Ask me any time you have questions," Lydia responded quietly.

"I don't think Mother would want me to learn anything without her approval. She is afraid that I will get confused. I better not ask anymore. She might find out and not let me come visit you. Oh! We forgot to write the invitation for me to come on baking day," Melody whispered.

"Let's just see if everything is okay at your home. We can send over an invitation tomorrow, once we recover from the storm," Lydia suggested.

As they neared Melody's lane, they met Jackson driving the carriage. He almost ran into them in the dark. "Oh, Miss Melody. Your mother is so worried. The tornado took off part of the roof and the house is damaged. Your mother is ready to leave tonight for a safer place. She sent me to find you. We have to leave tonight for Grand Island to stay with your aunt until your father hires someone to fix the house. No one could talk her into waiting until morning."

Melody climbed into the carriage. "Thank you Mrs. Jensen. I hope I can come back soon," Melody said through her tears.

Back home with her family, Lydia reported the whole story to Miriam and Anna. "Melody won't be back for some time. She needs our prayers. I fear that if her mother knew that we prayed and read the Bible, she would never allow Melody to visit us."

It was a sad evening for the whole family. Aaron prayed for the families that had lost their homes and loved ones in the storm. "We will see what we can do to help those less fortunate tomorrow."

"Why did you bring us out to this terrible place, Father? We didn't have tornadoes in Kansas City. Now the storm has ruined our tree and Melody's home and all those other homes. I don't like it here. Now Melody has gone, maybe forever!" Miriam sobbed.

"Miriam, God protected us in the storm. We had storms in Kansas City and before you were born, there was a tornado which destroyed many homes. This is the place where God has led us and He will take care of our needs," Father reminded gently.

Miriam looked up from her crying to see tears in her father's eyes. That surprised her. She had never seen him cry. "Is Father hurting, too?" she wondered.

"We've all had a very difficult day," Lydia reminded everyone. "I know it has been tough to leave your friends, Miriam. Anna also had friends and Jessie had playmates. We all left someone special. Now the tornado has damaged many homes. We can help others in their need."

"But I want to help Melody and she's gone! Why couldn't God have protected her house so she could stay here? Now I will never, never see her again. This is a terrible, miserable, detestable place." With that outburst, Miriam ran to the bedroom and fell onto her bed.

Later, Lydia slipped into the room. "Miriam, can we talk? There is something that you need to know."

"Mother, please don't tell me that God will take care of us and that this is such a wonderful place, 'cause it isn't, and no matter what you tell me, you won't convince me."

"I'm not trying to convince you that it is a wonderful place. But I do want you to know something. I was a lot like you when I was your age. I complained about everything. I made Mother very unhappy with my complaints. I know she was praying for me the day she died because I overheard her from my bedroom. I wish I could tell Mother that I have learned a little about not complaining," Lydia explained sadly.

"Mother, I never hear you complain. You always seem so happy about our new home and town. You mean you don't like this place either?" Miriam asked incredulously.

"It has taken me many years to learn that God knows best. It may not be what I like, or want but He knows the whole picture. It is not my place to complain because really I am complaining about what He has planned for me," Lydia answered quietly.

"Oh, Mother, thank you for telling me that you understand. I thought no one in the whole world understood how unhappy I was." Lydia pulled Miriam to her with a big hug.

"Let's get some sleep. We have a big day tomorrow helping those who have lost everything in the storm." Lydia smiled as she left the room.

Miriam lay there thinking, as the rest of the family prepared for bed. "Dear Lord, I'm sorry for being so grumpy. Thank You that Mother understands, and bring Melody back real soon. I'm so lonesome for a friend."

CHAPTER FIVE

CHURCH AND
HELPING NEIGHBORS

THE JENSENS slept late the next morning. Aaron said, "I will walk around town following breakfast to see which families could use some help repairing their homes. As soon as I find out, I will return to take Miriam and Anna to deliver cakes and bread for those families."

"You mean that I should make more bread today? We only have half a loaf left from the bread that I made last week," Anna asked.

"Yes, Anna, you should start now. I brought home some fresh ground flour from Mr. Hummel's mill. Make sure that we have extra cakes and cookies to take to these families. With their homes destroyed, they won't have much food or be able to bake. Thankfully, it is warm weather so they have time to rebuild," Aaron commented as he put on his straw hat for his walk around town.

Jessie said, "Can I go with you, Father? Miriam and Anna never take me anywhere."

"Yes, Jessie, you may go. Your happy smile will encourage them. Put on your bonnet. That sun will be hot by the time we return," Aaron replied.

Jessie ran for her calico bonnet with its large brim. It covered her small face in shade but she loved it. "It's just like Miriam's!" she had exclaimed when Lydia had finished sewing it for her.

Miriam and Anna were busy all morning baking bread and cakes. Lydia made some pies with some of the canned apples she had saved from last year. "It is so hot in here. Why couldn't other people take food to these people? Miriam complained. "I would have rather gone with Father."

Lydia reminded her, "Miriam, we should be thankful that we have a house with a roof after the storm. There are many families in town who can't use their homes for cooking or sleeping. As soon as your father returns, you can go with him to deliver the food. That will take you away from this hot stove."

When Father returned, he announced, "I just met the preacher, Rev. John Lockwood, from the Methodist Episcopal church. He moved his family here from Salina. He told me that he has found Beloit to be a very pleasant town. He said that the town has grown much since people started locating here in 1868. His children are thankful for having a school since some of them are in high school now. Their farm buildings were damaged some from the storm, but Rev. Lockwood is out comforting families who lost loved ones.

"How many families lost their homes? We have food ready to take to them. Are you going to take us in the wagon?" Miriam interrupted.

"Slow down! One question at a time. There are three homes completely destroyed. Some log cabin homes lost roofs, but the limestone homes right beside them stood solidly. And yes, I will take you in the wagon. Did you think I would make you walk and carry all this bread and the cakes?"

As soon as lunch was finished, Miriam and Anna donned their bonnets and packed the food in baskets. "We're ready, Father," they called to Aaron, who was hitching the horses to the wagon out in the yard.

One of the homes destroyed was near where Melody lived. "Look!" Miriam exclaimed. "There are workmen all over the roof of the Cramton's house. Where did he find so many carpenters when the other families need roofs also?"

"Maybe 'cause he is the mayor and has money," Anna suggested. "I bet her mother wanted it fixed instantly."

"Now, girls, we don't know any such thing. Remember we prayed that God would help the Cramtons come to know Him and the sooner they get their house repaired, the sooner they will be back in town," Aaron reminded them.

The girl's food was received with thankfulness. Anna said, "That was worth all the slaving over that hot stove this morning. Can we take some more tomorrow?"

"Tomorrow is Sunday and we are going to church to hear Rev. Lockwood. Now that we are finally settled into our home, we need to be in church," Father said.

That afternoon, Mother heated the flatiron on the stove and pressed all their dresses. Miriam heated the water for bathing the little girls. The galvanized tub was brought in from the back porch. Emma cried, "But I don't want a bath. You get soap in my eyes and it hurts. I want Mommy to give me bath."

"Hush, Emma, Miriam does a good job with your hair if you hold still. I have to get these dresses all pressed so I can make your rag curls before you go to bed."

Once baby Tabitha, Emma, and Jessie were bathed, Miriam carried the water out to the flower bed and put more water on the stove for Aaron's bath. She, Mother and Anna would bathe after they finished curling everyone's hair. It would be late when they finished.

Early the next morning, Aaron called Miriam and Anna, "Come girls, your mother needs help with breakfast so we can arrive at church on time."

"Father, will there be any children our age?" Anna asked. "I didn't see many children when we delivered the food yesterday."

"I don't know who comes to church, but Rev. Lockwood has several children," Aaron answered.

Once the little girls were dressed, their hair brushed and the hair ribbons in place, Miriam and Anna could dress. Aaron entertained Tabitha and Emma so Lydia could clean the breakfast table and dress. Emma said, "I'm scared to go to the church. Does Rev. Lockwood growl?"

"What do you mean does he growl?" Aaron chuckled, "I'm sure he is a nice man. He works on his farm and milks his cows just like the other farmers here. I'm sure you will like him."

Once in the wagon, the little girls settled down to watch as they drove the four blocks to church. Many wagons were already there with the horses tied up in front. Miriam spotted it first but Anna was the one who exclaimed, "That looks like the carriage that Melody's father owns. Why would it be here this morning? I thought they were in Grand Island. I didn't think they would go to this church."

Anxious to see if Melody was back, Miriam and Anna jumped from the wagon and were running into the church when Aaron called, "Girls, you forgot to help your sisters from the wagon. Each of you take one with you. Your mother and I will bring Tabitha."

Inside the small wooden building, Miriam and Anna looked all around the dimly lit room for Melody. She was sitting there beside her father in the front row. She turned around to see Miriam walking in the door but quickly turned back around. Miriam noticed that Melody's eyes were red and tearful. The church organist was pumping away at the song *Onward Christian Soldiers,* so they found seats as quietly as possible.

Rev. Lockwood's message was from Psalms 119 about God being a comfort in affliction, and that His word gives life and hope. Many of the families who had lost their homes and family members were there, some for the first time. Rev. Lockwood greeted them with special words, "We all grieve with you at your loss. It is only God who gives the comfort and strength during a time like this. God works through others to help meet those needs. After church today, there will be a meeting of all the men to plan how we can rebuild and repair homes following the funeral services tomorrow.

After the service, Melody walked by holding onto her father's arm. She wouldn't look at Miriam and Anna. Her eyes were still red like she had been crying. Anna whispered to Miriam, "Why is she back here? Surely they haven't gotten their house repaired this quickly."

Miriam shrugged her shoulders. She couldn't figure it all out. "Wish we could talk to her."

After the men had talked over plans to help with the rebuilding, the Jensens went home to a late lunch. "I'm thankful we have some fresh tomatoes from the garden and some of Mrs. Smith's eggs boiled for lunch," Lydia explained. "I know you are all starved. We have some pie left from the baking yesterday so that will finish our meal. Then we can all take long naps to recover from this difficult week."

"Do I have to take a nap? I'm not a little girl anymore," Miriam complained.

"You may read a book as long as you are quiet," Lydia suggested. "The rest of us need rest."

Once the house was quiet, Miriam tried to concentrate on her book, but all she could think about was Melody. "Maybe I could walk over there to see if she is at the house. No one will miss me for an hour or more." With that thought, she slipped quietly out the back door.

At the Cramton's lane, Miriam was surprised to see men working on the house. "Don't they know this is Sunday?" she wondered, "No one else is working on their house today."

Nearing the house, she couldn't decide if she should talk to one of the men about Melody, but that was answered with Melody bursting out of the house crying.

"Melody, what is wrong? Can I help? Why are you here when your house is still in a mess?" Miriam asked as she ran to hug her friend.

"You can't help. No one can. Father says I must go stay with Mother in Grand Island. I hate that place. Can I come stay with you until the men repair the house?" Melody begged.

"It would be awfully crowded. Do you think your father would let you stay with us? He doesn't know us."

"I refuse to go back to Grand Island. Father will just have to let me stay here then. My room wasn't damaged, and the roof is almost finished. Here he comes now. Let me ask him if I can stay with you. That might convince him to let me stay here," Melody conspired, her tears forgotten. She knew how to persuade her father to see things her way.

"Father, may I stay with the Jensens while the men finish the repairs?" Melody asked sweetly.

"Who are these Jensens? Your mother would never allow you to stay with strangers. I am sending you back to Grand Island with Jackson this afternoon. I should have never allowed you to come with me," Mr. Cramton grumbled.

"But Father, I can help you with the paper. Couldn't I stay in my room? It isn't damaged." Melody purred with sugar sweet words that she knew her father couldn't resist.

"Very well. I will have Jackson send a message to your mother. Now, who is this young lady here with you?"

"Father, this is Miriam Jensen. She is my new friend. She is very intellectual." Melody explained coyly.

"Well, Miss Jensen, do come in for a visit. I've got to get back to the men. See that you girls stay here where I can find you," Mr. Cramton said bruskly.

"Didn't I tell you that Father would do just what I

wanted? He never seems to notice that I have disobeyed him if I tell him just the words he wants to hear. He needs my help on the paper and he wants me to spend time with intellectuals so you must sound intellectual when he comes around," Melody chuckled.

"What will you do here all day? Won't you be bored here alone all day? You can't stay at his office all day," Miriam questioned.

"Oh, I will think of something. Why don't you come visit me tomorrow and we can make some plans. I know lots of places to meet some handsome boys," Melody joked.

"Mother wouldn't let me go meet boys. Remember we are only thirteen!" Miriam looked shocked. "I had better run home. Mother doesn't know that I am gone. I must be in my room before anyone wakes up. I will see if I can come tomorrow afternoon."

"Sneak off if your Mother won't let you come. I'm free to explore the city after I help Father in the morning. We can have fun. Maybe if you brought Anna, your mother would let you come bring me some cookies. Then we can send Anna home," Melody suggested.

Walking home, Miriam was thinking, "Mother may think I complain a lot but at least I don't try to trick her like Melody does her father. I will just have to keep telling Melody about God and praying for her to come to know Him. I know Mother and Father would want me to do that."

Everyone was asleep when Miriam slipped into her room. "That was simple and I was able to help Melody. She needed me," Miriam convinced herself.

CHAPTER SIX

BARN BUILDING AND MRS. CRAMTON

EARLY THE NEXT MORNING, Aaron was up before sunrise. While Lydia fried salt pork and eggs, he gathered his hammer and saw. "I hope that you have a big turnout to rebuild the Smith's barn," Lydia said. "They need that barn with all the cows they milk. Do you have any idea how many men plan to come?"

"No, Rev. Lockwood just said to get the word out to everyone. Mr. Smith said they usually have twenty to thirty men, so it goes fast."

Eating hurriedly, Aaron mumbled between mouthfuls, "Have the girls bring over jugs of cool water by mid-morning. It will be hot by then. We will need lots of food and water to keep going."

Lydia asked, "Do you know who planned the meal? Nellie Brown asked me to bring four pies, but she didn't say who had told her what to bring."

"No, I don't know, but everyone helps around here. They love an excuse to get together. One of the men said yesterday, that once we get the houses and barns rebuilt, they will probably have a barn dance. Told me to get my fiddle tuned up for some square dancing music. I don't remember telling anyone that I played a fiddle. Wonder how he knew?" Aaron mused.

Lydia was working on the pies when Miriam came into the kitchen, "Where's Father? I didn't know he was leaving so early."

Lydia answered, "The crew wanted to start early before the sun got hot. He asked that you and Anna bring cold jugs of water to the workers by mid-morning."

"But Mother, Anna and I wanted to walk to Melody's to see if she was still there. She might be gone if we wait. Did you see her crying when she left church?" Miriam complained. She decided there was no reason to tell her mother about her visit yesterday.

"I'm sorry, but that will have to wait. Rebuilding homes and barns is our number one priority now. Maybe after we feed the men, you and Anna can visit Melody."

Anna stumbled groggily into the kitchen, "Why didn't you call me, Miriam? You said we would leave early for Melody's place so that we would be sure to catch her."

"Father said we must take water to the men working on the Smith's barn," Miriam moaned. "By the time we do that it will be time to help with the noon meal or take care of Emma and Tabitha so Mother can help. Mother said that we could go after the men are fed."

"But she might leave before then," Anna whined. "She might even go back to Grand Island. Please, Mother, can't we go now?"

"No, you can not go now," Mother interrupted. "You must dress and eat so you can take the water. We can pray

50

that if God wants you to talk to Melody, she will still be there this afternoon. Hurry now. Your father will be unhappy if you are late."

The twenty men made fast progress on the Smith barn. Mr. Smith had brought in several wagon loads of lumber from Timothy Hersey's mill. Everyone was grateful for Mr. Hersey's help to build the town. He had built the mill on the Solomon river near the bridge in 1870. Mr. Hersey had been the first mayor of Beloit. He was the one who suggested the name of Beloit after Beloit, Wisconsin where he had lived in his younger years.

By noon, the men had the barn all framed and were ready to lift the heavy beams for the roof support. Wiping sweat from his brow, Mr. Smith asked the women, "Could we have dinner now before we start this heavy lifting?"

Lydia and the other women proceeded to bring all the food to the planks which had been placed across saw horses, under the oak trees that had withstood the storm. Miriam said, "I can bring your pies over here while Anna watches Emma and Tabitha." Her mother nodded and continued visiting with the other women. She hadn't met many of them before so this was her first chance to get acquainted.

The men washed up at the well and Mr. Smith said, "Now we will have grace. Rev. Lockwood would you talk to the Lord for us?" After the "amen" was said, the men grabbed plates and loaded them high with fried chicken, ham, homemade bread, fresh corn on the cob, green beans with salt pork, and mashed potatoes with milk gravy. Aaron whispered to Lydia, "Where are your pies? I want to be sure to get a piece. They all look good but I know that yours is the best." Lydia smiled at his compliment.

"This is the best part of the whole disaster," Mr. Smith said. "This good food makes everything go better, and the help of all our good neighbors makes the work go faster. This barn is going up much quicker than when I built it six years ago. Next, we will rebuild the Johnson's barn. They almost have their house redone with the help of neighbors last Saturday."

The women and children ate after the men had finished. Lydia had Miriam and Anna take the little girls back to the house for naps. "As soon as I help clean up, I'll be home. You and Anna can leave then to visit Melody."

"But Mother, that may take an hour. You said we could leave after the men ate. Can't the other women clean up? We have been waiting all morning," Miriam complained.

Lydia looked stern, "I'm sure Melody can wait that long. She doesn't know that you are coming. I must help the women clean up so they will be ready to serve again tomorrow." Miriam was thinking, "There's no use telling Mother that Melody is waiting for me. That would require explaining how I knew."

Grumbling all the way, Miriam and Anna found Emma and Tabitha with Jessie, under the oak tree, playing in the soft dirt. They didn't want to leave, but Miriam said, "Come on girls. Mother said that you have to take your naps."

"But we want to play in this nice dirt. We don't have this nice soft dirt at our house. We can take naps later," Jessie complained.

"No, come on so Emma and Tabitha will come." They took the hands of each of the younger girls and started for the house. Jessie followed grudgingly.

"Look at your dresses and your hands," Anna said. "They are filthy. Come here and let me wash your face and hands. Mother won't let you take naps being that dirty." After she had washed them and changed to clean dresses, she took them to their beds.

Jessie was still complaining about leaving their nice soft dirt, "Why don't we have dirt like that here? It is so nice to play in. Couldn't Father get us some dirt like that?"

Miriam started to explain, when Mother came hurrying in. "I'm back girls. You can leave now. It didn't take long to clean up with all that help, but it was so hot washing dishes. Would you bring me a cool drink from the well?"

Anna took the bucket and turned the windmill loose to let the wind pump water from the well. She filled the bucket and pulled the handle down to stop the windmill. She was thinking, "When Father gets our barn built, we can have a big tank of water for the cows to drink, and for us to play in to cool off in the summer. I can't wait." She carried the water back to her mother.

Miriam was waiting impatiently outside the front door, "Come on Anna. I have your bonnet. Let's hurry." Anna ran to catch up with Miriam who was already down the lane.

Once out on the road, the girls almost ran to Melody's house. "Oh, I hope she is still there," Miriam said puffing as she ran.

As they walked up the lane, they could hear hammers; the men were still at work. "They must not be done with the roof yet. Look at all those men up there. How does Mr. Cramton get so many men when almost all the men in town are working at Smiths?" Anna questioned.

"I don't know, but why don't you pull the knocker or we will never find out if Melody is here," Miriam remarked. Within a few minutes, Jackson, who had brought Melody to visit them, opened the door. "Is Melody here?" Miriam blurted. "We have come to see her. We wanted to come this morning but we had to feed the men."

Without any emotion Jackson said, "She is in her room. I will tell her you are here. I don't know if she will see you." He marched off towards the bedrooms.

"Oh, I hope she will see us. It must be terrible to have trouble and not have anyone to talk to; I just know we could help her," Anna wailed.

"Don't worry about that, she wants to see us, and remember what Mother said, "If God wants us to help her, He will work it all out."

Jackson came back promptly to report, "She said she will be out in a few minutes." He walked off without another word. The girls sat in silence, looking around the room.

"Their house doesn't look damaged very much. It looks just like it did when we were here last time. I wonder why her mother won't come back now," Miriam said.

Melody came quietly into the room, dressed in a beautiful pink batiste dress. At first they didn't know she had come. She was so quiet. Suddenly Anna looked around and exclaimed, "Oh, Melody, we came to help you. Have you been crying?"

"Don't mind her, Melody. She forgets her manners. What do you want to do this afternoon?" Miriam asked, looking sternly at Anna.

"I do need to talk but we can't talk here. Come outside with me. I will tell Father that we are going for a walk. He wants me to get out more anyway," Melody whispered. They followed her outside where she told her Father, who was supervising the work on the roof.

"Be back by six, Honey, so I won't worry about you," Mr. Cramton reminded her.

"We will, Father," Melody answered sweetly.

Melody didn't say a word until they were out of sight of the house. "I can't allow Jackson or the cook to hear anything, or they will tell Mother. Follow me, I have a hide-away where we won't be heard." They followed her into thick woods near the house to a cool and dark little cave in the side of a hill. "This is where I come when I need to think. But it is no fun to come here by myself. I need to talk to someone. I am so troubled," Melody announced once they were inside.

The girls found seats on the rocks and waited for Melody to explain. "I don't know where to start. I suppose you saw that I was crying yesterday. Father tells me that crying won't fix anything, but I don't know what else to do. When we were staying with my aunt in Grand Island, Mother told Father that she was never coming back to this town. She said she hates it and if he insists on staying here, she will stay in Grand Island. Father's work is here with the newspaper and I love it here but Mother wants me to come live with her. I feel like they are tearing me apart. Father needs my help at the newspaper since he has trained me in typesetting since I was a little girl, but I can't bear to leave Mother with all her problems. What can I do?" She started to cry softly.

"I don't know what the answer is, but I do know that

God wants your parents together," Miriam responded. "Father read verses to us from somewhere in the Bible about God hating divorce. But that won't make your parents stay together. Have you thought about praying about it Melody?"

"I don't know much about praying. We learned some prayers at church but they aren't much help with this problem," Melody answered. "I learned more from Rev. Lockwood's sermon last Sunday than I had from any other church. I wish we could go all the time. Father said that he liked it also."

"I wish you could talk to Mother, she knows a lot more than I do on problems like this. Would you like to talk to her? We could go there right now if you want," Miriam suggested.

Melody didn't say anything for awhile. "I would like to talk to your mother, but I don't think I should be gone any longer, or Father will be asking questions. He probably wouldn't mind, but Jackson and the cook would tell Mother if I asked him. I wish they didn't work for us, but Father can't cook and I can't do the washing, so we have to have them. Why don't I see if I can visit you tomorrow. But now I want to talk to you alone, Miriam. Could you go on home, Anna?"

"Well I guess, but I'm not sure Mother would like it if I come home without Miriam," Anna remarked.

"Just tell her that I needed some extra time with Miriam, and I will come talk to her tomorrow." Melody begged.

"All right, but Mother won't like it, so you had better be home soon Miriam," Anna reminded her.

As soon as Anna was out on the lane, Melody whispered, "Now follow me. We can have some fun. Have you ever been to the Ice Cream Palace? There are all sorts of cute boys there." She giggled, seeming to forget about her problems.

"Mother wouldn't want me talking to boys like that. She says that a proper girl doesn't talk to boys," Miriam protested. "Can't we just stay here and visit?"

"Aren't you my friend? I want to go. If you don't come, I am going alone," Melody pushed.

"If Mother or Father find out where I have been, they won't let me come visit you anymore," Miriam said.

"They won't find out unless you tell them. Don't you want some of that special ice cream? They have so many different flavors," Melody insisted.

"I'll go this one time, but we must be back by supper time so that I am home before Father arrives," Miriam agreed unwillingly.

Once away from the house, Melody said, "Let's run so we will have lots of time." She gathered up her beautiful long ruffled skirt and took off so fast that Miriam couldn't keep up.

Breathlessly, they arrived at the Ice Cream Palace. Once inside, Melody called to the many boys and girls in the room. "I want you all to meet my new friend, Miriam. She has never tasted this good ice cream. We need to show her the fun we have here."

Miriam could see that Melody knew everyone there. She kept thinking, "Mother wouldn't want me here."

"Come Miriam, let's try the latest flavor of fresh peach ice cream. Do you want a soda also?" Melody enticed.

"I didn't bring any money. Just give me a small soda."

"I'm treating, so you can have anything that you want. We can sit here with William and Isaac. Move over boys. My new friend is a little shy." Melody laughed loudly.

The ice cream was delicious. Miriam exclaimed, "I've never tasted anything so good. Wish I could take some home to Anna and the rest of the family."

"Oh! You can't do that. This is our secret place. If you take some home, they will know where you have been," Melody smiled secretly.

Finishing her ice cream, Miriam stood up and said, "Look at the time. It is 5:30 and Father will be home at 6:00. We must run, or he will be looking for me."

Melody paid for their food and they ran out the door. "It must be terrible to have parents who won't let you have a little fun. I know of some other places that are lots of fun. If you can sneak away some afternoon, I will take you again."

"I must get home right now. You promised your father that you would be home also. Come tomorrow and talk to Mother. She can help you with your problems." Miriam didn't want to hear about Melody's fun. She felt guilty already for sneaking off. After leaving Melody, she ran all the way home.

Anna was helping Mother prepare supper, and telling her of their visit with Melody. "Mother, could she talk to you tomorrow? She said she would see if she could come tomorrow. I know you can help her more than we can. I don't know what we would do if you left Father," Miriam interrupted.

Lydia looked surprised. "Where have you been? I

expected you to be here earlier. And as for your father and me getting a divorce, you don't need to worry about that. Your father and I made a promise to stay married for life. I think Melody's mother has many other problems. We need to pray that God will show us how to help the whole family. Now would you set the table before your father arrives?"

Miriam didn't say anything about her visit with Melody. She was thinking, "If Mother knew where I have been, she would never let me go again. How can I help Melody see that I don't want to go with her to the Ice Cream Palace?"

The men had Mr. Smith's barn almost done by nightfall, and by the next afternoon, they were ready to start on the Johnson's barn. "Looks mighty good, boys. Just right for a barn dance when everyone's home is rebuilt," Mr. Smith said.

Aaron arrived late for supper, but Lydia had kept it warm in the warming oven on the stove. "Thank you, Miriam and Anna for keeping the water ready for the men. They all remarked how helpful you girls had been today."

Anna grinned at Miriam, "Yes, it was good to help."

The next afternoon, while Emma and Tabitha were napping, there was a quiet knock on the Jensen's front door. Lydia was startled because she hadn't heard anyone arrive. At the door, was a frightened Melody who looked like she had been running. "Oh, Mrs. Jensen, can I come in? I need to talk to someone right now."

Lydia led Melody to the kitchen, and poured her a drink from the bucket. "Here, drink this and get cooled off before talking," she said. Miriam and Anna left their reading to come into the kitchen also. All sat in silence while Melody regained her composure.

"Mrs. Jensen, what am I going to do? Father told me this morning that I have to decide where I am going to live by tomorrow. He has to stay with the newspaper since that is his work but he told me that if I wanted to live with Mother, he would train someone else to do the typesetting that I do. I don't want to make that choice. He said that Uncle George was bringing Mother from Grand Island tomorrow to pick up her clothes and some of the furniture. If I am going to live with her, I will have to leave then," Melody was crying by then, quiet little sobs.

Lydia prayed silently for the right words to share with Melody. "Melody, that would be a very difficult decision to make. My mother died when I was your age, so I worked with my father for several years before he died. That decision was made for me. Your decision is much more difficult. Is there any way I could talk to your mother when she comes tomorrow?"

"It wouldn't do any good. She won't tell anyone her problems. She complains to us, but to others she pretends she doesn't have any problems," Melody said sadly.

"Would you be willing to let Mother try talking to your mother?" Miriam asked. "Maybe if we prayed real hard, something would work out so that your parents would get back together."

"I had better go home now. Father doesn't know that I left. If Mother agrees to see you, I will send a message over with Jackson tomorrow. I will ask the cook to have tea ready, and tell Mother that we have a special visitor coming. I don't know much about praying, but I know that you do. Would you pray real hard that God will change Mother?"

"Melody, when you are a child of God, He hears and answers your prayers," Lydia answered. Some of the answers will be 'yes,' some 'no' and some 'wait,' but He always answers. You can become His child anytime."

Changing the subject abruptly, Melody said, "I think I had better hurry home before anyone misses me. I will see you tomorrow. It might be better if you came alone to see Mother."

"Yes, Anna and Miriam will have to stay with the younger girls," Lydia agreed.

After Melody left, Mother said, "Girls, when your father comes for supper, we need to pray specifically for the Cramton family. Only God can change people."

They did pray following supper, and after everyone was in bed that night, Miriam saw her mother sitting at the table with the Bible. She knew she was asking God for the right words to share with Mrs. Cramton. She felt guilty for not telling her mother the whole story of her afternoon. "I've never kept anything secret from her before. But if I tell her, she won't let me go to Melody's," she contemplated.

The next day, Lydia and the girls made pies for the men working at the Johnson's, and Miriam took them over, but the women told Lydia that they could handle the meal. They knew that she had her hands full with the little ones.

"Do you think Jackson is coming with that note? It is two o'clock already," Miriam questioned. They were reading quietly while the little girls slept. Hearing horses in the drive, they looked out to see Jackson jump down from the carriage. He knocked on the door and handed Lydia a note on fancy paper, and stood waiting while she read it.

"Ma'am, I'm supposed to bring you in the carriage if you are ready to come. Mrs. Cramton has arrived and is waiting to meet you," Jackson stated.

Lydia wasn't quite prepared for a carriage ride, but reached for her bonnet and her small Bible. "Pray for me, girls, and give Emma and Tabitha some cookies and milk when they wake from their naps."

Jackson drove without a word and delivered Lydia to the front door of the Cramton's home. "She's waiting for you, Ma'am. Just go on in."

Lydia didn't know what to expect, but opened the door to find Mrs. Cramton sitting in a wheelchair right by the door. "You must be Mrs. Jensen. Sorry I can't get up to greet you. Melody has told me much about you."

Lydia laughed nervously, "I have enjoyed visiting with Melody. You have raised a very gracious daughter. She cares so much for you."

Mrs. Cramton motioned for a chair and called, "Olive, you can bring the tea now. How long have you lived here in Beloit, Mrs. Jensen? It is such an uncultured town; I don't know why I ever agreed to move here. I'm here to pick up my clothes and some furniture. I've found a house in Grand Island."

Lydia finally was able to answer her questions. "Call me Lydia. We have been here for three months. I have found the people so friendly. They help each other. It wasn't like that when we lived in Kansas city."

"You left Kansas City to come out to this deserted

62

place? How could you leave such an interesting place with all that culture? I would think you would want that for your girls," Mrs. Cramton asked.

"Mrs. Cramton, my husband wanted to come here to help people with his blacksmithing ability. My place is with him. Yes, it has been difficult getting our home settled, but we are happy being together as a family. God has taught me many lessons about being content in the circumstances where He puts me."

"Mrs. Jensen... Lydia, how can you be content? This life must be miserable compared to Kansas City. God has never done anything for me. He let me have this terrible accident which made me unable to walk. How can He care anything for me to leave me a cripple for the rest of my life?"

"Mrs. Cramton, I know being unable to walk must be very difficult, but God loves you very much. So much so that He sent His only Son, Jesus, to die for you. If you will believe in Him, He can help you learn to be content even when you have problems," Lydia answered prayerfully.

Mrs. Cramton was almost in tears, "No one has ever told me that before. Where did you learn this?"

"From God's word, the Bible. If you would allow me to, I could teach you some of what God has taught me. Would you be willing to stay here for a few weeks so that I could share with you from the Bible? I still have much to learn, but I would be glad to share with you what I have learned."

Mrs. Cramton sighed deeply, "Yes, I will stay for a few weeks. If you can teach me how to be content when I will never walk again, it will be worth staying in this town."

"I must return home now. The girls will need help with supper. Shall I come tomorrow afternoon?" Lydia asked.

"Yes, I will call for Jackson to take you home and he will pick you up tomorrow."

Lydia was rejoicing when she walked in the house. "Guess what girls? Mrs. Cramton has agreed to allow me to share with her how to be content when she is crippled for life. God did answer our prayer that she would agree to stay. At least for awhile she will be here."

"Maybe the whole family will come to believe in Jesus, and she will stay forever. I'm going to pray for that," Miriam said.

CHAPTER SEVEN

THE BARN DANCE

THE REBUILDING of houses and barns was progressing well. After two weeks of steady work, Aaron came home after one long day to announce, "Tomorrow should finish up the last barn. I've asked the men if they would build us a small barn after that. We need our own cow and some chickens."

Anna said, "Oh, goody, goody. Then we will have a tank."

They all turned to look at her. "Why do you want a tank? Are you a cow?" Jessie laughingly asked.

"No, but I want a place to cool off on these hot afternoons," Anna answered.

"Mr. Smith said that since we are almost done with the rebuilding, he is inviting everyone to his place Saturday night for a barn dance. He also told everyone that I would be joining the men with my fiddle. I've never played for a barn dance. In our home we only sang church songs. I don't know if...," Aaron reported.

Lydia interrupted, "From talking to all the women while we served the meals, it sounds like everyone comes to the barn dances. They are a part of every wedding, housewarming or holiday. All ages come, from children to the elderly. Usually they have food beforehand. They all come in their Sunday best. I danced some when I was a girl, but I don't know what they dance here. I think we should go. It sounds like a fun way to meet our neighbors. It's Mr. Smith's way of thanking everyone. I'm sure the other fiddle players will teach you the music. You play so well by ear, it wouldn't take you long to learn."

Miriam and Anna couldn't wait to talk. "Could we invite Melody? She would love it."

"I mentioned inviting the Cramtons to Mr. Smith. He said that they have never come to any event in the community. He was sure that Mrs. Cramton was not happy here," Aaron answered.

"Maybe while I am teaching Mrs. Cramton from the Bible this week, I can mention the barn dance. She might surprise everyone. She certainly has been receptive to all that I have shared with her," Lydia said.

Melody came over the next morning while the girls were helping Lydia with the washing. Miriam was scrubbing the clothes on the wash board while Lydia rinsed them in another tub. Anna hung them on the line. Melody asked, "Can I help? I need to learn how to wash clothes. Olive won't let me help her."

"But you have on your Sunday dress, you can't get it all ruined," Miriam objected.

"No, this is my everyday dress. Mother insists that I wear nice clothes every day. Some days I would like to wear an old dress and be comfortable," Melody answered. She walked over to where Anna was hanging clothes. "Here let me help you. I know that I can put clothes across a line."

After the washing was on the line and the wash water was poured on the garden, Lydia and the girls poured cool drinks from the well and sat in the shade to cool off. Emma, Tabitha and Jessie were happily playing with the new kittens that Mrs. Smith had given them.

"Melody, did you know that Mr. Smith is having a barn dance Saturday night? Would you like to go with us?" Miriam asked.

Melody looked worried, "I couldn't. Mother will not allow me to go to any parties that she doesn't plan. I really would like to go, but I know there is no use asking her."

"What if your mother and father came? Would they let you come with them?" Anna asked.

"I'm sure they wouldn't come, so there is no use of me hoping that I could come. Mother thinks that barn dances are so crude. She grew up in Chicago where they had a full orchestra for dances every week. I know she wouldn't go to a barn for any kind of party," Melody said sadly.

Jackson came with the carriage to deliver Lydia for the Bible study with Mrs. Cramton. Once inside the house, Lydia found Mrs. Cramton with her own Bible opened on the table. "Oh, Mrs. Cramton, I'm so thankful that you have your own Bible. Now you can follow while we read."

"You can call me Mary," Mrs. Cramton said. "Let's stop being so formal. I had Olive dig through my cedar chest to find my childhood Bible. I haven't read it for years."

They studied through the first chapters of John. Olive brought them tea after an hour of study. "Thank you for teaching me so much. I am so ignorant on religious things. You seem to know God like He is your best friend."

"He is, Mrs. Cram... I mean Mary. I accepted His payment for my sins when I was a young girl. Knowing God is in control of everything that happens, helped me through the time when my mother died."

"I didn't know that your mother had died. Did your father remarry after that?" Mary asked.

"No, he died a few years later and I moved to Kansas City to live with my grandmother. That is where I met Aaron," Lydia answered.

Lydia stood up, preparing to leave. It was then she remembered the barn dance at the Smith's. She said, "Mary, Melody would like to attend Mr. Smith's barn dance Saturday night. They are inviting everyone to celebrate the rebuilding of the homes and barns."

Mary frowned, "I couldn't let Melody go without us. I have always been very cautious of the people Melody spends time with. She is a very talented girl, so I don't want her attending some crude affair in a barn."

"Well, that certainly is your choice. I'm sure Melody would be safe with our girls. Aaron and I would be with her also," Lydia suggested.

"I trust you, but not others in this town." Changing the subject Mary said, "I know that you must be tired after your busy day. Can you come again tomorrow afternoon?"

Lydia chose to walk home. She needed to think. She didn't want to push Mary into spending time with others in town, but felt it would be good for her to get out of the house.

Every day that week, the mornings was spent with Miriam and Anna helping Lydia sew new calico dresses for the girls to wear to the barn dance. As they worked,

Miriam asked, "Do you think that Mary will change her mind and allow Melody to go with us Saturday night?"

"I haven't mentioned the barn dance since that first time. I don't want to upset her. It is more important for Melody's mother to learn about God, than for Melody to go to the barn dance. There will be lots of parties for Melody other times. If her mother can see God's love for her, it might change a lot of things for Melody."

Lydia walked to Mary Cramton's that afternoon. She had told Mary that she enjoyed walking after being in the hot house all morning. After a light knock she walked in to find Mary smiling. There was something different about her whole attitude. "Come right in. I want to show you something," Mary said. "Last night I was reading the first chapter of John that we had studied and it suddenly came to me. Those verses about becoming a child of God by believing in Him; well, now I do believe that He died for me. At last I see what you have been trying to show me. I have been religious all these years but I didn't really believe in what Jesus had done paying for my sin. How can I ever thank you for helping me see that. I feel as if a load of guilt has been taken off me. I know my sins are forgiven."

Lydia reached over and hugged Mary tightly, "I'm so glad you understand that. It wasn't me who did it, but God who showed you from His word. That's why He says His word is sharper than a two-edged sword. It points out our sin. The angels in heaven are rejoicing that you are now a child of God."

It was a joy for Lydia to teach Mary more about her new relationship with God. As they were finishing the study, she asked, "Have you told Melody and Mr. Cramton about becoming a child of God?"

"Oh no! I wouldn't dare. They wouldn't understand," Mary exclaimed.

"You might be surprised how much they understand. I think you should share it with them as soon as possible. I'm sure they have already seen the change in you," Lydia smiled.

As she walked home, Lydia thanked God for answering her prayer for Mary. "Lord, help Melody and Mr. Cramton also to become Your children."

Miriam and Anna were finishing their dresses, hemming by hand the long ruffled skirts, when Lydia arrived home to tell them the good news about Mary. "Did you say anything to Melody's mother about her going to the barn dance? Maybe now that she is a Christian, she will not be so uppity," Miriam said.

"I'm not going to say anymore about it. She knows when and where it is. I want choices like that to be hers," Lydia answered.

"Well, I am going to pray that God will change Mrs. Cramton's mind. He has changed her a lot already," Miriam said.

Saturday night came. Lydia and the girls had been baking pies and frying chicken all day for the picnic. They packed all the food in a basket, along with their dishes and silverware. "Now, girls, help me dress Jessie, Emma and Tabitha. Your father will be home soon and we need to be ready to leave."

The Smith's yard was beginning to fill with horses and wagons as people from all around Beloit began to arrive.

Everyone was dressed in their Sunday best. Mr. Smith had cooked a whole hog for the picnic, so he was busy cutting it up for the meal. As Aaron walked up, Mr. Smith asked, "Did you bring your fiddle?"

"Yes, but I don't know anything except church songs," Aaron answered.

"Oh, you'll soon learn. This music just grows on you. They all love *Turkey in the Straw* to start the square dancing. Jim McIntosh will be doin' the callin' tonight. He really gets some action."

The planks across the saw horses were almost sinking under the load of food. Mr. Smith was ready to ask Rev. Lockwood to say grace, when a carriage, pulled by black horses and driven by Jackson, came pulling into the lane. Folks whispered, "It's the Cramtons. They've never come to one of our affairs before."

Mr. Smith marched right up to the carriage and greeted the Cramtons. "Welcome to our picnic, Thomas. Can we help your wife into her wheelchair? I have just the place for her in the shade of the tree."

Everyone made way as Mary Cramton, smiling gaily, was pushed to the shade of the tree. Melody was following behind until she spotted Miriam and Anna. She was dressed in a beautiful lacy green dress with ruffles all down the skirt. She hurried to join them. "Can you believe it? My mother coming to a picnic. I've never been to a picnic in my life." She was almost to cry with joy.

"That's a be-e-e-utiful dress, Melody," squealed Anna as she looked down at her own simple calico.

Miriam grabbed her arm, whispering, "Sh-h-h, we're getting ready to pray."

71

"Now, we will have Reverend Lockwood say grace, and start on all this good food," Mr. Smith announced in a loud voice.

There was much visiting as they ate under the trees and around the yard. Mary and Thomas Cramton seemed to enjoy visiting as much as anyone.

Following the meal, Mr. Smith announced, "Get your dancin' shoes on. We're going to start the squares just as soon as the men get their fiddles out."

Aaron nervously tuned his fiddle and headed for the barn. The other men were tuning their banjos and mandolins along with several fiddles. At least he wouldn't be alone.

Jim McIntosh started calling, "Get your partner. Ladies in the center, gents round 'em run. Swing yer rope, cowboy and get yo' one!" It wasn't long before several squares of couples were dancing to the music. Aaron caught on quickly.

Jim, the caller, said after an hour of square dancing, "Can you guys play some slower music and give my throat a rest?" They went through several waltzes and the Virginia reel.

Melody whispered to Miriam and Anna, "This is a lot more fun than my parties. They are always so stuffy. We just pretended to have fun. They are really having fun here. But can't we go outside for awhile? I saw William and Isaac out by the wagons."

"Father would want us to stay inside," Miriam answered.

"He won't even miss you. Look, he is concentrating on his music. And if he does, he will probably think you've gone to the outhouse. Come on," Melody begged, pulling on Miriam's arm.

"Just for a few minutes so Father doesn't come looking for me," Miriam muttered as she followed Melody out behind the barn. "It's dark out here. How can you see?"

Outside, some young guys were teasing young Jake Howell about going with the new school marm. "Bet your kisses sound like a cow pulling her foot out of the mud." That did it, Jake grabbed the teaser by the collar and pounded him with his fist. Jake was big and strong from hard work on the farm. The other young guys yelled, "Give it to 'em, Jake." But soon they were yelling, "That's enough Jake. Keep him alive." The fight stopped just as soon as it started and they all went back inside to finish up the last of the square dancing.

The girls found Isaac and William watching the fight. Isaac saw them first. "Oh, hello Melody. I didn't see you standing there in the dark. What are you girls doing out here? This is no place for girls, but now we're glad to see you. Let's go for a walk. The moonlight is terrific," Isaac exclaimed.

"Give me your hand, Miriam, I'll help you around the wagons," William requested.

"No, I'm going back inside. My parents would not approve of this. Come on, Melody, let's go back inside." Jerking her hand away, Miriam gathered up her skirts and headed back inside. She thought Melody was behind her, but turned to see Melody walking towards the creek holding Isaac's hand.

Lydia looked up from her visiting as Miriam walked back inside. "Where is Melody? Weren't you with her?" Lydia asked. "Her mother is still not convinced about barn dances for her daughter. We must not worry her any."

"But Mother, I couldn't get her to come back inside. I-I-went with her as she asked. I told her that Father wouldn't approve of me leaving the barn. But she wouldn't listen," Miriam explained.

"Where is Melody now? Mary was asking about her a few minutes ago," Lydia asked.

"She won't like me telling you, but she is walking with Isaac, a friend she meets at the Ice Cream Palace." Miriam didn't tell her mother how she knew this. She was sure her mother wouldn't understand.

"Is there something you are not telling me, Miriam? We must find Melody right away. Come with me and show me where she is. We must not worry her mother." Grabbing Miriam's hand, she hurried out into the night. "Lead the way and pray that we can find Melody before her mother finds she is gone."

"I heard Isaac say that he wanted to walk down by the creek. How can we find them in all those trees?" Miriam said breathlessly as she ran to where she left Melody.

Leaving the wagon area, they rushed to the edge of the woods around the creek. "Melody, Melody, this is Lydia. You need to come back inside right now," Lydia called.

"Melody, Isaac, William can you hear us? Please come back," Miriam called.

Faintly in the distance, they heard someone calling, "Help! Melody has fallen into the creek. We're bringing her." Miriam and Lydia could hear loud noises coming from the woods, and someone crying.

"Oh, I hope she isn't hurt," Lydia exclaimed. "We'll have to take her over to our house to change her clothes. Pray that Mary hasn't missed her."

Isaac and William emerged from the woods half carrying Melody between them. She was soaked to the skin. "Oh, Mrs. Jensen," she cried, "what is Mother going to say?" She fell into Lydia's arms.

"Come with me Melody. We have to change you into some dry clothes. You boys may hear from Melody's father on this," Lydia said sternly as she marched Melody over to the house. Miriam held on to Melody's arm as they silently walked past the barn.

"Mrs. Jensen, please don't tell Mother what happened. I promise I won't do it again. Miriam told me not to go but I wouldn't listen. Please don't tell Mother or she will never let me spend time with Miriam again. Please..." Melody begged.

"I don't know, Melody. From what Miriam told me, you have visited with Isaac and William before without your parents' permission. If you were my daughter, I would want your mother to tell me. I will have to pray about this. Meanwhile, let's get that dress off. Thankfully you can wear one of Miriam's dresses, but I don't know what you will tell your mother happened to this beautiful dress. I'll let you take care of that," Lydia admonished.

Once Melody was changed and her hair combed, they walked back to the barn. Mary looked up in surprise as Melody walked in, "Where have you been? I've been asking people if they had seen you in here," Mary asked.

"Oh, Mother, I tripped going to the outhouse and tore my new dress. Lydia helped me change into one of Miriam's dresses," Melody lied to her mother without looking at Lydia.

The hour was late and people were loading up their

wagons and carriages for the trip home in the moonlight.

Walking home after the dance with a full moon shining through the trees, Lydia said to Aaron, "That was the most fun I have had in years. I didn't know a small town could have so much fun. And to think that the Cramtons have missed it all until tonight. God is answering our prayers for them. I wonder if Mary has forgotten all about moving to Grand Island? She is going to need all the help we can give her with Melody."

"Why do you say that, Lydia? I thought she and Miriam were having fun square dancing with the other boys and girls. They seemed like proper young ladies."

"I'll explain later, Aaron. We need to pray for Melody and Miriam's friendship. Miriam needs a friend but I'm not sure Melody is the right kind of friend. I don't know what to do. I'm sure Mary wants Melody to spend time with Miriam — especially now that Mary has become a Christian — but I'm not sure Miriam can handle Melody's strong will," Lydia sighed as she held Aaron's arm as they walked across the field.

CHAPTER EIGHT

INDIANS AND MELODY'S DILEMMA

THE NEXT MORNING, Aaron called Miriam from her bed early before anyone else was awake. "Miriam I need to talk to you. Can you come quietly so as not to wake your sisters?" Miriam could tell that something was bothering her usually tranquil father.

"What's wrong, Father? Have I done something to displease you?" Miriam asked timidly.

"Not that I know about Miriam, but there is something I need to share with you. Your mother told me about the incident outside the barn with Melody and the two boys last night. She is fearful that Melody is leading you into dishonesty with your parents. Is there anything else she has asked you to do that you knew would not be acceptable with your mother and me?"

"Well-l-l, she did take me down to the Ice Cream Palace without permission. I knew you would not want me down there talking to the boys but she was so insistent, just like she was last night. What can I do? I want to be her friend and to be able to show her how Christians live, but it seems to be more and more she is pushing me to do things her way," Miriam said sadly.

"You are correct in thinking that, Miriam. From now on, when she suggests going somewhere that you know we do not approve, tell her that your father absolutely disapproves of it. Melody is a very spoiled only child, used to disobeying her parents, so it will be difficult for you to say no to her. I know that you can be trusted to obey my orders.

"But what if she tells me she will no longer be my friend unless I go someplace with her to meet Isaac and William or whatever?" Melody questioned.

"You are to tell her that you must come right home, and do just that. If she sees you mean it, and she still wants to be your friend, she will not push you to disobey us. Your mother and I are praying about telling her parents what happened last night. I'm sure they are not aware of how far Melody has gone to get around them," Aaron cautioned.

"She told me that a girl must meet lots of boys so she will know the right one to marry. I want to tell her about courtship, and how you and mother will guide me in choosing the right husband that God has for me, but I think she would laugh at me. We are too young to marry, I don't know what her hurry is," Miriam confided.

"I must get to the shop, Miriam. Your mother and I will be praying that God will guide you in your friendship with Melody. You also must be praying that God will help you to be the right kind of friend. Sometimes the best friend is the one who will say 'no' when wrong choices are being made." Aaron gave Miriam a hug and left for work.

Lydia came out of the bedroom, "Did I hear voices out here? Why are you up so early, Miriam?"

"Father asked me to get up early so he could talk to me about Melody. I didn't realize how she was pushing me into things that you and Father have forbidden, until he showed me. She was convincing me to not tell you what we had done, knowing that you would not approve. How can I continue being her friend? It makes me angry just thinking how she pushed me to disobey you," Miriam fumed.

"You can be sure that your father and I will be praying for you, and Melody and her family. They need our help, and Melody needs Christ to change her life. You can still be her friend without doing everything she wants. You might be surprised to find that once she sees you will not disobey us, she might follow your example. Let's start breakfast before the girls wake up. Your father left without breakfast; he must have been troubled. Would you want to take him some homemade toast? I'll start repairing Melody's dress before I go to Mary's for Bible study this afternoon. She may have ruined that new dress, but at least we can wash and mend it."

Miriam made the toast and buttered it with fresh butter from the Smith farm. With her bonnet in place, she walked out into the beautiful summer morning. She found Aaron hard at work at the blacksmith shop while visiting with Mr. Smith. Mr. Smith was saying, "Did you lose much business while you were helping us rebuild the barns? I know that your family has to eat. When you have some time, I would like for you to rebuild this wagon that was damaged in the storm. I'll pay you well for the job — 'cause you do a mighty good job with your 'smithing."

Old Mr. Hansen came hobbling in and sat near the door, chewing his tobacco and spitting outside. Miriam found him repulsive, but her father had told her about his interesting stories. This time she would hear them first-hand. "Did you fellers ever hear the story about how our first mayor was captured by the Indians when he was livin' in Abilene? During the civil war he was appointed Indian trader. One day while he was prospecting for tin ore, he was captured by Pawnee Indians and held for three days. That same year, 1859, Cheyennes chased him fifteen miles in an attempt to cut him off from his encampment, and kept him under constant fire. He was wounded eight times by arrows. The Indians also stampeded his stock and burned his hay stacks."

Aaron exclaimed, "I'm sure glad things are more civilized today. That would be too much excitement for me. Mr. Hansen, do you know of anyone who had good visits with the Indians around here? Surely they were not all bad."

Mr. Hansen spat out the door and thought a long minute. "I heard tell of a young boy over in Jewell county who was out in their farm house with his papa when a band of Indians all dressed in their war paint arrived in the yard and walked straight into the house. They didn't even bother to knock. Mr. Clark was shocked, but that little Laddie Clark was delighted. He had long golden curls which bounced when he laughed.

"For some reason, Mr. Clark excused himself and left the little guy with the Indians. The savages got the grand tour of the house by Laddie. He showed them his new top his grandma had given him. They laughed when he made it spin. He showed them the stockin' his mama was making him and all his father's clothes. The Indians laughed and said, 'Huh.' Laddie tried to say it the same way, so they helped him say it right. He wasn't the least bit scared of those savages. Can you imagine that?

"Laddie got out his Bible pictures of stories his mama was teachin' him, and told them about Daniel in the lions den and how the lions wouldn't eat him. He also showed them savages about Jesus blessin' the little ones. The Indians said, 'huh.' Next he showed them Jesus dyin' on the cross. This time they didn't say 'huh.' They just got up and left the house in a hurry."

"Yes, there were lots of good Indians and some became Christians. I remember a story about two young girls who were captured by Indians from a home near Beloit and taken out of town and left. A preacher and others found them alive and brought them back, but their mother died from all the shock," Mr. Smith continued.

"Help me remember all these stories to tell your sisters at noon, Miriam. They have been asking me if Indians are still around here," Aaron remarked.

Aaron went home for dinner and was repeating the stories for the girls. Miriam said, "Well, Mrs. Smith told me about a girl in Leavenworth. They say she was combing her hair by a window and in her mirror she saw Indians who were coming into her room. She screamed and ran into the other room. I would too. Mrs. Smith said there was an army man there and the girl could barely speak to say, 'Indians.' The army man found the Indians laughing, saying they wanted to see her hair, but she wasn't about to go back into the room."

"Well, Mr. Hansen said that he has a picture of Indians who visited in Beloit in the '70s. They usually just wanted some handouts but they never bothered to pay or knock before coming in. They were fascinated with white man's food and houses and often just came to look," Aaron concluded. "I wonder if Melody knows these stories," Miriam asked. "I bet her mother would leave town for good if an Indian would show up at her door. Melody said that her mother liked the barn dance, but she still has problems living here."

"Yes, even though she has accepted Jesus as her Savior, she still has struggles," Lydia said. "She thinks that Melody won't get the musical training she wants for her. She was talking about sending her to Chicago to live with her aunt, to attend a special boarding school for girls. They teach all sorts of musical training and drama. I didn't know what to say when she told me that."

"But Melody wouldn't want to leave her parents and go that far from home. Has her mother even considered what Melody wants?" Miriam asked.

"I try to stay out of their family problems," Lydia ventured. "I'm there to study the Bible with her and to allow her to ask questions about it. If she wants my opinion on the idea of sending Melody to boarding school, I will tell her that she is better here with her parents. But she hasn't asked me."

Anna, almost in tears, said, "She can't leave. She just can't. She's lots of fun. It's fun teaching her things like baking bread and pies that the cook won't allow her to do. Why would her mother be so mean as to send her away? What can we do to stop her?"

"We can pray that God will help her parents to see that the best place for Melody is with them," Aaron answered softly. "I just heard that a new music teacher came to the school. I'm sure that he would give lessons."

"You could give her violin lessons, Father," Miriam suggested. "You were the best fiddle player there at the barn dance. I heard the men saying that."

"Yes, I could teach her a few things, but I can't read music and I don't have training in music. I am afraid that her mother wouldn't consider me a good teacher of music."

"Let's pray right now for Melody and her parents," Lydia interrupted, "that God will give me wisdom to know what to share with Mary this afternoon when we meet to study."

Mary seemed upset when Lydia knocked lightly on the door for their Bible study. "Come in," she said tearfully. Lydia hurried to her side.

"What is wrong, Mary? You've been crying. Is there anything I can do?" Lydia asked.

"Melody has been very unhappy ever since I told her that we are sending her to boarding school in Chicago. This afternoon she was so angry that she ran out of the house and has not returned. I don't know where she is. Her father is in Kansas City on business so he can't help Jackson look for her. Jackson came back telling me that there are Indians camped outside of town. He said that he didn't like the looks of them. He wondered if they might have captured her. If only Thomas would get home. We must leave this town as soon as we find her, if the Indians haven't captured her and taken her away. I can't stand living here knowing that Indians can come into town. What am I going to do? I thought that once I believed in Jesus, my problems would be over," Mary cried.

"If I gave you that idea then it was my mistake," Lydia answered softly. "Becoming a child of God is like starting life as a baby. You learn to trust Him with your problems as you learn more about God and His word. We will always have problems until He takes us to heaven. He uses the problems to shape us to be like Christ. Do you want me to go for the sheriff and have him look for her?"

"Oh no! Just think how that would look if they found out that we had been arguing, and she was right here on our property. I'd never be able to face people again," Mary answered. "I have so much to learn. Thank you for being patient with me. What are we studying today?"

"Are you sure you feel like studying? If you want me to, I can go look for Melody, or I can have Miriam and Anna come look for her. I know they talked about a cave that was in the woods near here," Lydia suggested.

"Let's study first. I need the help from God's word. It gives me peace when I read and learn. Would you read to me from Psalms? I have found them so comforting."

Lydia read several Psalms. She could see Mary relax. "Would you like to pray about Melody now?" she suggested.

"I have never prayed out loud. You pray and I will silently."

Following the prayer, Lydia said. "Why don't I go home and have Miriam and Anna come look for Melody. She might allow them to find her when she wouldn't let Jackson." She walked to the door and opened it. Mary stopped her with a question.

"Do you think we are doing the right thing to send Melody to this excellent boarding school in Chicago? She could live with her aunt. She would be able to take the train back every holiday."

Lydia sent up a quick prayer for wisdom, "Mary, she is your only daughter. I know that you want what's best for her but, if she was my daughter, I would want to train her myself. There are more important lessons than music lessons, that only parents can teach. That is why I am teaching our girls at home this year. They could go to the school here, but I want them to have a strong foundation from the Bible, and I want to know the teachers here before I send them. I don't know if that answers your question or not. We can talk more about this during the lesson tomorrow, if you would like."

"Thank you, Lydia, for being honest with me. I felt that since I was in a wheelchair and couldn't take her to lessons and events myself, that I should send her to the best schools money could buy. I didn't think about her need to be with us. Just pray that we will do the right thing."

"Mary, you can be sure that I will be praying. Now, I must go help find Melody, to let her know you want to talk to her. I am sure that you have some areas to work out with her."

Lydia almost ran home. Walking briskly up the lane, she thought she heard laughter out by the barn. She hurried to the north side where she found Miriam, Anna and Melody playing with the three little girls in the cow tank. "Girls! What are you doing? Do you realize that Melody's mother has been almost sick with worry about Melody?

Give me Tabitha, and all of you must get out at once and change into some dry clothes. Melody, I need to talk to you as soon as you are dressed."

"But we were having so much fun. Melody thought it was the most fun she has had in ages. She don't want to go to no girls school She told us so," Anna argued.

Lydia couldn't keep from laughing at Anna's use of words, "We will talk about that as soon as you are dry and dressed. Now come on inside."

Once the girls were dressed, Lydia had Anna take the younger girls into the sitting room. "I want to talk to Melody and Miriam in the kitchen. You entertain the little girls with the story book we found at the library last week."

Melody looked worried. "Are you going to scold me for running off from Mother?"

"No." Lydia assured her. "You already know that you did wrong. I want you to know that your mother is trying to do the best for you. I'm sure you don't see it that way."

"Then why is she sending me off to this old girls school, and to live with stuffy Aunt Fannie? I know I would hate it there. I want to stay here and go to school with your girls. Why won't she let me do that?" Melody pleaded.

"Melody, it may not seem like it but your mother loves you very much. She is a new child of God and is learning many things about finding His plan for her life and yours. All parents make mistakes. We are not perfect. Right now, you need to go home and tell your mother that you are sorry for running away."

"But, I am not sorry. I wanted to make her see that I

will not go away from here. She wouldn't listen to me tell her. Daddy is no help either. Whatever mother says, he does. What good will it do for me to talk to her?" Melody asked.

"I think you will find your mother will be willing to talk. Try it. We will be praying for you as you go home. Remember that God loves you very much and wants your best. When you become His child, you will understand that even better," Lydia answered.

Melody left rather unwillingly. Her hair was still wet. Her beautiful dark curls were hanging limp down her back. Lydia prayed that Mary wouldn't scold her for playing in the tank with the girls.

"Can't God make Melody's mother change her mind? Melody was so much fun playing in the tank. She acted like a normal girl rather than a fancy dressed-up party girl. Her mother won't let her have any fun," Anna said.

"Yes, God can make Mrs. Cramton see that Melody would learn more by staying with her family," Lydia answered. "We need to give God time to work in the Cramton family. Remember, Melody and her father have not become children of God yet, and that makes it hard for her mother to work things out God's way."

Well, I'm glad that both you and Father believe in God and we pray about plans before we do anything," Miriam said. "I thought God made a mistake sending us here, but now that we have met Melody, I think this place is even better than Kansas City."

"Yes, girls, God has given you a wonderful father who wants to obey God. You may not always be happy with his decisions, but some day you will be grateful," Lydia reminded them. "Look at the time! We need to find some supper for your hungry father who will be arriving soon. After supper you can help me mend Melody's dress so I can return it to her mother tomorrow. You should have given her an old dress for playing in the tank."

CHAPTER NINE

THE SALOON EXCITEMENT AND MELODY'S DECISION

MELODY WALKED slowly home that evening. She didn't want to face her mother. She knew she would be angry for causing her so much worry. Melody hadn't known the Indians were camping near town. All she had thought about was escaping from her mother's demands. "I just wish she could see that I don't have to be trained to be a concert pianist. I just want to stay right here," Melody muttered to herself.

Once at the house, Melody opened the door quietly. She found her mother with her head bowed, praying quietly, "O, Lord, bring Melody back. I'm so sorry to have driven her away with my demands. Don't let anything happen to her. I love her so much." Melody tiptoed out the door and came around to the back door so she wouldn't disturb her mother. She prepared a glass of tea and took it to her mother.

"Mother, I'm home. I'm sorry for causing you so much concern. I was with Anna and Miriam the whole time. I didn't know about the Indians. I can't stand leaving here, so I just had to get away."

Mary reached to pull Melody down to her and hugged her tightly. "I'm sorry too, Melody. I didn't realize that my demands that you get the best education were not really the best. Lydia helped me to see that. Your father may not agree that you can get a good education here in Beloit, but I will talk to him. We all need to reconsider these things. He will be concerned about the Indians also, because he had an item in the paper just this morning about Fleetfoot, a Cheyenne Indian, offering fifty ponies for the return of his daughter who had eloped with an army deserter at Wichita. I know you wouldn't do anything like that, but I don't trust the Indians. I wish your father would arrive soon. Do you remember what time his train is arriving?"

"I think it was around five this evening but the train could be late. He told me that sometimes there are antelope or cattle on the track that stop the train until they move on, unless one is hit and that takes longer."

Jackson took the carriage to meet Thomas on the train, but Harold, Thomas' reporter from the newspaper, was waiting already. "Have to get the boss right away. There's an exciting story that we need to get in the paper tonight. Carrie Nation and her WCTU women led a raid on open saloons in Beloit today. They were singing *Onward Christian Soldiers* and carrying hatchets to the saloon on the west side of Mill street. The owner and the men opposing Carrie Nation were prepared. They had a fire hose connected to a hydrant to turn on full force on the women. But one of the women of the WCTU asked, probably forced, her husband to slash the hose with a razor.

"When the men yelled 'turn 'er on,' Mr. Caddes slit the hose, and instead of a gush of water it was a tiny trickle. The women rushed inside the saloon and loud crashing noises could be heard. In little time, a small trickle of liquor could be seen running down the side of the street. Every bottle, mirror, keg of beer, and any other breakable thing was broken or destroyed.

"They arrested Mrs. Nation later, but she had the money to pay her bail. The saloon owner says she bankrupted him, and he will never reopen."

Thomas heard the story as Harold drove him to the newspaper office. "Yes, this story must be on the front page, even if I have to stay until midnight. Go pick up Melody to help set type, Jackson." Jackson had followed to remind Thomas that supper was waiting. "And tell Mary that I will be late."

Thomas and Melody arrived home near midnight. As they rode home in the carriage, Melody asked, "Father, I really would like to stay here in Beloit for my schooling. Mrs. Jensen told me that the new music teacher knows many instruments and does give lessons at the school. Can't I just stay here? I don't want to go to Chicago to that boarding school."

"I'm too tired to talk about such serious business tonight, Melody. Your mother and I have given this careful consideration and know that you would get the best schooling at the girls finishing school in Chicago. They have a wonderful reputation, and my sister would see that you were given the best dance, piano and elocution lessons money can buy."

"But Father, there are other things a girl should learn in addition to music and public speaking. Please...."

"Not another word. Your mother and I will talk this over tomorrow. Now we both must get some sleep."

The morning paper that was delivered to everyone's doorstep caused quiet a stir. Aaron was reading it to the family when Miriam stopped him. "Why do those men drink that awful stuff anyway? Mrs. Smith was telling me a remedy to cure hard drinking. Her father gave it to her. He said that it really works. It cured him. She said you gather Roman wormwood in the full of the moon when it is in blossom, while the dew is still on it in the morning. Dry it and make it bitter by placing it in water. Drink frequently and when you are faint. You must continue this one year and it will deliver you from the desire of ardent spirits. Mrs. Smith said wormwood is so bitter it almost makes a person vomit, so that must be why it works."

"Any person who has to have strong drink to make them forget their troubles, doesn't know what God can do for them," Aaron said. "Maybe if they would come to the revival services they are having every night at the Methodist church, they might be converted and give up their drinking. That would close all the saloons without Carrie Nation taking her Women Christian Temperance Union all over the state."

Lydia came into the kitchen with a worried frown on her face, "Jessie has a high temperature and has a deep cough. I am really concerned. One of the neighbor women told me that whooping cough is going around. Aaron, would you bring me some tar from the barn? I need to make a cough syrup for her. I have the red pepper and horehound and ginger but I don't keep tar in the kitchen. Just bring a spoonful. That's all I need. It will take some time to boil this down, so I had better start the water heating. Mother always used the cough syrup for us when we were little."

Lydia tried to keep Jessie isolated from the younger girls to keep them from catching the whooping cough. "Wash your hands girls, anytime you are around Jessie. Miriam, could you take turns with Anna reading to her. She wants to get out of bed, but if someone is reading to her she rests quietly," Lydia requested.

"But Melody said she was coming today. Shouldn't I go tell her not to come?" Miriam asked.

Just then, Melody knocked at the door and walked in. Lydia exclaimed. "Melody, you shouldn't be in here. Jessie has whooping cough. I know that your mother would not want you to be here."

Melody backed out of the door and Miriam followed. "I'm sorry that we can't visit. Mother needs me to read to Jessie so she will rest quietly. I hope this doesn't last long.

"Is Jessie very sick? Mother worries about my health all the time. She will be upset to know that I walked in the house with Jessie sick. I should have waited until you came to the door. I love to come to your home, I never thought there would be any problem. Can I bring some books for Jessie? I have bunches. Couldn't you visit with me outside when I come back?" Melody requested.

"I'm sure Jessie would enjoy more books and probably I can visit with you outside. Mother said that whooping cough can be very bad. Maybe your doctor has something to keep you from getting it," Miriam said.

Melody walked home sadly. She wasn't looking forward to fourteen days of not visiting Miriam and Anna.

Mary was upset when she heard that whooping cough was going around. "I almost died of that when I was a child. We must send Jackson to Dr. Antrobus and Dr. Home above the Beloit bank. Their homeopathy medications I trust more than some of the others medications advertised. He might have something to keep you from getting the whooping cough, or to keep it from becoming so serious. Call Jackson for me."

"Is it all right if I take some of my books for Miriam to read to Jessie? Can I visit with Miriam outside?" Melody asked.

"If you take books, don't ask for them back. They will be covered with germs. I suppose it would be safe for you to visit with Miriam outside but whatever you do, don't go inside," Mary insisted.

Jessie's fever continued for several days. Her terrible cough kept everyone awake at night. Lydia's cough syrup helped some. After ten days, she was beginning to improve, and asked to eat, but she was still a sick little girl. Anna woke up one morning complaining of a headache. Lydia felt her head. "Oh, no, you are coming down with whooping cough. Go back to bed and I will bring the onion and garlic compresses for your chest. Maybe with the cough syrup and that we can keep you from being so sick."

Melody continued to come each afternoon to visit with Miriam outside. "Father is still insisting that I leave in September for Chicago. He will not listen to Mother or me

96

about my going to school here in Beloit. He will not even talk to the school board, or Professor Culver, the principal, about how the school is run. He is so stubborn about me having the best musical training. I would just like to learn to cook and sew like you. Besides, I don't want to leave Isaac and William. Couldn't you ask your father to teach me the violin like he has taught you to play the violin? Father was impressed with his playing at the barn dance. We've got to make Father change his mind."

"I have been praying all along that your father would change his mind. You are my best friend, and I know you would only be home on the holidays if you leave. But if your father said you must go, you must obey him." Miriam was thinking that Melody thought pestering her parents worked better than praying, but she knew it was no use to argue with her.

"I won't go. I'll run away first. It is a terrible long ride on the train alone. He told me that he wouldn't have time to ride with me, and mother isn't able to travel. I sure wouldn't want Jackson to go. What am I going to do? It is only six weeks before I have to leave."

Melody didn't come the next afternoon. Jackson came with a note from Melody. "I have whooping cough. Can you come see me? I feel terrible, but since you have been around it with your sisters, Mother said you could visit me."

Miriam asked Lydia, "Can I visit her, Mother? I'm worried about her. She says she always gets very sick whenever she has some sickness. She hasn't accepted Christ. If anything would happen to her…. What can I tell her about believing in Jesus so she knows she will go to heaven?"

"The easiest verse in the Bible is one Melody may

already know. John 3:16 explains it all. Let's stop right now and ask God to use you to share that with Melody." As they prayed, Miriam started to cry.

"Mother, I'm afraid that Melody might die. I'm so scared something will happen to her. She is my best friend. She told me this week that we had to think of some way to make her father change his mind about her going to Chicago. She doesn't want to leave Beloit. I think it has something to do with Isaac and William, not just because we are friends. Yesterday, she asked if Father could teach her to play the violin. I know her father wouldn't allow her to learn from someone who doesn't have a music degree. What are we going to do? I am afraid I will start crying when I visit her."

"God will help you to be strong while you are there. And He will guide you on the right things to tell her. You know that I will be praying for you. Don't stay too long. She will be weak and needs to rest. You know how the coughing wears your sisters out."

"Can I take some of your cough syrup to Mary for Melody? Maybe Mary would want to try it. I know it sure has helped Anna and Jessie."

Lydia poured some cough syrup in a jar. "Tell Mary what the ingredients are so she won't worry about it's safety."

Miriam prayed as she walked to Melody's. "Dear Lord, I'm so scared for Melody. She doesn't know You. I may not be very good about telling her. I don't want her to die. Please help her get well."

Jackson answered her knock. "Come right in. Melody has been asking for you, but Mrs. Cramton didn't want to

bother you." Miriam was surprised to see Jackson so concerned about Melody.

Mary heard her voice and called from the bedroom, "Miriam, is that you? Come back here. Melody has been begging me to send Jackson for you." Miriam walked into the large room with the beautiful canopy bed. Melody looked so small and pale in the huge bed of pink ruffles and lace.

"Mrs. Cramton, I brought some of mother's homemade cough syrup. It has horehound, ginger, red pepper and a little tar. It helped Anna and Jessie to be able to sleep. It also let us sleep when they weren't coughing all the time."

She sat on the chair beside the bed. Melody was so hot that the maid was bathing her with cool clothes. "Miriam, thank you, thank you for coming. I kept begging Mother to send for you." She started coughing and couldn't stop.

"Bring me a spoon, Anabel." Mary insisted. "Maybe this cough syrup will work better than the Chamberlain Cough Remedy purchased at the Morris Drugstore." Once Melody had swallowed a spoonful, her cough eased and she could talk.

"Mother, could you and Anabell leave and let Miriam and me visit alone? She can call you if I need help," Melody whispered.

Once the door was shut, Melody said, "I'm so scared Miriam. Dr. Antrobus said that I had a very bad case of whooping cough. I can tell Mother and Father are very worried. Mother prays all the time when she thinks I am asleep. I'm afraid to die, but when I asked Mother to tell me how to get to heaven, she started crying and couldn't talk. Can you tell me?"

Miriam couldn't keep back the tears but she started

in, "Do you know John 3:16? I learned it when I was a little girl. You do believe that God loves you, don't you?"

Melody nodded her head. "I know that I've done wrong things. Mother talked to me about learning that all of us are sinners. That was a surprise to her because she thought she was a good person. What do I have to do?"

"You don't have to do anything, Melody. Just tell God that you believe that Jesus died for your sins. You can do that right now."

"Will you pray for me. If I talk very much I will start coughing which will bring Mother and Anabell running."

Miriam prayed and Melody whispered "Amen" at the end. "Now we are both God's children." She smiled. "I'm going to tell Father when he comes home. He is so worried about me. I'm going to tell him that if I would die, I will go right to heaven."

"He might not understand that, Melody. Since he hasn't accepted Christ like you and your mother, it might upset him," Miriam reminded her.

"I'm going to tell him. He needs to accept Jesus too. Then our family could read the Bible together like your family does every evening. I just love being with your family. You all seem so happy. Fancy homes and money doesn't make people happy. I know, 'cause Father buys me anything I want. He told me that when I get well, he will take me to the Kansas State Fair in Wichita."

"But, I saw in the paper that it was in September. Aren't you to be leaving for Chicago before that?" Miriam asked.

"Father is changing his mind about that. I've heard him and Mother talking when they thought I was asleep.

He was so worried about me that he sleeps on the floor by my bed. God is answering your prayers for me. Now Father is talking about me attending the Beloit normal school. He met Professor Culver on the street yesterday, and asked about the classes and teachers. I think he will let me stay here at least for this year."

"I must go, Melody. Mother said to not wear you out or make you talk much. I can come back tomorrow. I'm so glad that you are now a child of God, and maybe you will stay here all year. Just hurry and get well."

Melody weakly waved goodbye. "Come tomorrow. I must sleep now. I am so tired."

Miriam stopped to talk to Mrs. Cramton on the way out, "Melody asked me to pray with her to receive Jesus. She was afraid to die. Maybe you can teach her some of what Mother taught you. I'm not very good at explaining things like that."

Mary started to cry, "Oh, thank you Miriam. I couldn't keep from crying when she started talking about dying. Maybe now I can handle talking to her about the Bible lessons. Come tomorrow and read to her if your mother doesn't need you. You have been an answer to my prayer today."

Miriam almost skipped home. Two of her prayers for Melody were answered. Maybe, with Mary and Mother praying with them for Mr. Cramton, that one would be answered also.

During supper that night, Miriam reported her exciting news about Melody. "Do you suppose now that Melody has accepted Jesus she will stop lying to her parents and sneaking out to see Isaac and William?"

"Accepting Jesus is just like being born as a baby. Melody has much to learn about God and what it means to walk in obedience to Him. You can help her learn these things. Just because we are God's child doesn't mean that we are suddenly perfect," Aaron reminded her.

"But what about all the lies she has told her parents? Should I remind her about them?" Miriam asked. "I'm sure her mother thinks Melody's salvation means she will be a nice obedient Christian girl."

"It doesn't work that way, Miriam. They both have to learn to obey God step by step. God will convict her about her lies. Melody will have to unlearn her bad habits of disobedience and lying to her parents. That will take time, and she may have some real heartaches until she learns. Remember, you have known the Lord for several years; you will have a big responsibility to help her learn. It could be in tough love you tell her 'no' to something she wishes to do," Aaron admonished.

"Dear God," Miriam prayed that night after the family was asleep, "I don't think I can keep Melody doing the right thing. Help me from being tempted with her exciting ideas. She could get us both into trouble because our parents trust us. And help Melody to get well." With that, she finally dropped off to a fitful sleep.

CHAPTER TEN

THE CELEBRATIONS AND MELODY'S RECOVERY

MELODY SLOWLY RECOVERED. Miriam visited her each day, reading to her from the many books Melody had in her library. Their reading and talking was often interrupted with Melody's coughing spells, but those were becoming less and less. One afternoon when Miriam arrived, Melody was sitting in a chair in the living room reading the Beloit Gazette. "Listen to this. 'The Grand 3rd and 4th of July Celebration. Horse races, foot races, bicycle races and baseball. With the Flambeau Club and fireworks in the evening. The Manifold's Military band will furnish music.' You could win the bicycle race and win a lamp for your bicycle, Miriam."

"My bicycle wouldn't go that fast," Miriam responded. "Besides, they wouldn't let girls enter the race. I read in the paper that Justin Rodda rode his bicycle to Delphos last Sunday in less than three hours. That is 29 miles. I couldn't compete with that. Why should I do something like that? I want to stay here with you."

"I'm going to go. I can't stand another day in this house, even with you reading and visiting every day. I want to hear the band and see the fireworks. They have invited all the neighboring towns by reducing the rates on the railroad. Father wants Mother to attend the Grand Ball at Cooper Opera House that night. Since she can't dance anymore, she doesn't want to go. Even if she could dance, she has changed so much since believing in Jesus, I don't think she would go. She seems more interested in going to Bible study than cultural things. Father gets upset because she has changed so much. It must make him feel guilty or something. She asked if he would go with us to the Christian church this Sunday and all he said was, 'I guess, if it will make you happy.' I could see that he would rather stay home."

Miriam had to hurry home that day. Lydia had told her before she left, "I need you home to help with canning. Anna is feeling well enough to watch the little girls but I need your help peeling the tomatoes, or I will be all night finishing the canning."

As Miriam was leaving, Melody said, "I wish I could watch you canning tomatoes. There is so much I don't know about homemaking. Our cook doesn't do any canning. She says we can buy 3-pound cans of plums for 30 cents and tomatoes for 20 cents so why should she slave over a hot stove, canning. Jackson raises a garden, so we have fresh vegetables, but we have to give most of it away since we can't eat it all.

Back at home, Lydia and Miriam visited while they

worked. "I can't understand why Melody's father won't accept Jesus so he and Mrs. Cramton can pray about Melody going to Chicago and read the Bible together like we do."

"God doesn't push anyone to accept Him," Lydia responded. "Even with all of us praying for Mr. Cramton, God allows everyone to make their own decision to believe in Him. Some people wait for years. Some wait until they are dying. They miss out on the joy of walking with God during their life."

They had just finished the last of the canning when Aaron arrived for supper. "I found a buyer for your extra chickens, Lydia. They also want turkeys and geese. The New York store is paying six and seven cents a pound for turkeys, but only five and a half cents for chickens. A farmer brought some corn by the shop so I bought a wagon load for the calves at fifty-fife cents a bushel. We want a fat calf to butcher for our winter meat. Mr. Smith told me that he would help me butcher when colder weather arrives."

"I will be thankful for some fresh beef. The fried chickens have been great, but fresh beef would be a good change. Did you read the Beloit Courier today? Editor Caldwell has a great sense of humor. Not only does he constantly remind us that 'every Republican in northwest Kansas ought to subscribe' but this week his story was about the water main breaking on Mill street. Here, let me read it to you. 'The breaking of the water main has caused a good deal of speculation among the businessmen of that thoroughfare, whether it was caused by an upheaval of earth caused by gas or his Satanic Majesty peeking out of his den to see if his authority on sin was being disputed.' Can you beat that for interesting reporting?" Miriam laughed.

"His paper is always good for a laugh," Aaron agreed. "Did you see his note about the box supper last week? He said that it was quite enjoyable for those who like that sort of lottery business. The men who got the five cent ticket for some lady's lunch took her to the scales and paid one fourth cent for each of her pounds for the privilege of eating her box of eatables. He said 'one lady of pretty good natural weight smuggled a heavy cannon ball in her apron before stepping on the scales and amazed her partner by tipping the beam at over 300 pounds, but he paid the regular price.' He said there were not many guests but those who were there seem to have enjoyed the fun."

Miriam asked, "Can we talk about something serious? I am still concerned that Melody's dad is going to send her to Chicago. If he doesn't think the schools here are good enough, he may go ahead with the plan. She said he almost changed his mind when she was so sick. What can we do to convince him that Melody should stay with her family?"

"Nothing, Miriam. He is her father. We can pray for her and for Thomas, that he would make a wise decision. But if he decides to send her, we should not interfere."

Miriam said, "I'm going to pray all the time. Mr. Cramton just has to accept Christ, and see what is best for Melody."

The next day, Miriam walked to Melody's home. Melody answered the door herself. "Look, I am much better, and guess what? Father says he is taking me to the Kansas State Fair in Wichita, September 28th. I told him that I wanted you to go with us. He said he would think about that."

"But, I thought you had to be in Chicago right after

Labor Day. Did your father change his mind about you going?" Miriam asked incredulously.

"He never really said that he had, because I don't think he is convinced that I will receive the best musical training here, but my sickness scared him. I think he is even thinking about what would happen if he should die." Melody answered.

Miriam said, "God is answering my prayers. I couldn't stand having you leave."

"Mother said that I could sit out in the sunshine today," Melody said changing the subject. "I haven't been outside for so long that I don't know what fresh air smells like." They found chairs out in the flower garden that Jackson so carefully tended. Day lilies and roses were blooming profusely. "Oh it smells so good out here. I must tell Jackson thank you."

"I thought you couldn't stand Jackson," Miriam commented.

"Well, since I accepted Jesus, I started praying for Jackson, and I found he wasn't such a bad guy after all. He just needs to believe in Jesus, too."

"Did you really tell him that?" Miriam asked.

"Yes, I did and he told Father. Father told me to quit pestering Jackson with my religion. He said it was all right for Mother and me to be religious if we wanted, but to leave the rest of the household alone. Let's change the subject. Mother got this new magazine in the mail, and it has so many new styles and dainty cooking and etiquette. It comes out of New York for only a dollar a year. I want you to see the Delineator. I saw just the dress I wanted, and mother said that if the New York Mercantile has it, I can buy it."

"I've never had a store-bought dress," Miriam said. "Mother makes all of our clothes. It must be nice to go pick out any dress you like."

"But I would like to learn to sew like you do. I've never sewed on a button or hemmed a dress. You must be so proud when you wear something you have helped to make."

"Guess we should trade places for a month," Miriam laughed. "Wouldn't that be fun? I could go to the Opera House with your parents, and take trips to Kansas City and Chicago and to the fair in Wichita. That would be so much fun."

"I think I would have more fun in your family. I could practice violin with Anna, and take my schooling from your mother. And to sit around the table and have your father read the Bible every night. I could help your mother wash clothes and get to play with Tabitha every day. That would be more fun than traveling to Chicago. Riding the train isn't that much fun. It is boring compared to being with your family," Melody said wistfully.

"Let's ask our mothers to see if they would let us do that. I must get home. Maybe your mother will let you walk over to our place tomorrow afternoon."

Once at home, Miriam told Lydia about the idea of exchanging homes for a month. "Wouldn't it be exciting to live with the Cramton's. I could buy my clothes at the New York Mercantile and go to the Opera House every week. The Cramtons are going to Wichita to see the Kansas State Fair. Melody wanted me to go but I know you need me here to help. How could I be gone for two days?"

"You sound like me when I was your age," Lydia

smiled. "I wished things would be different. Since Mother had died and Father died when I was in high school, there wasn't much money for new clothes at Grandmother's house, but there was lots of love. She taught me so much about being happy with what I had. If you really would like to trade places with Melody, I will mention it to Mary to see what she thinks."

About that time, Aaron walked in for supper. "Guess who visited me at the shop today? Thomas Cramton said that Melody would like for Miriam to go to the Kansas State fair in Wichita, so he purchased tickets for all of our family to ride with them. He said that we would be gone for two days.

Lydia and Miriam received the news with excitement. Lydia exclaimed, "But what do we wear? We will have to have new clothes to go to the fair. I must go to James Harper's store to buy some of that beautiful percale for some new dresses. How will I get all that sewing done with the gardening and canning?"

"Hold on a minute. You might be interested in an item in today's paper. The New York Store is discontinuing business in Beloit. They have $50,000 worth of merchandise to close out at once. They are selling dry goods, clothing, groceries and shoes, and are buying chickens to be shipped out soon. With the sale prices, your extra chickens might buy dresses for all the girls. I see that women's shoes are 85¢. In the same paper the Famous Clothing House said that their clothing was water soaked from rain coming in the skylight. They are selling men's suites for a dollar. You won't have to spend your time sewing."

Miriam couldn't believe it. "We are really going to the

fair. I can't wait to talk to Melody. Now that her father is allowing her to go to school in Beloit, I can see her every day."

"Wait a minute, young lady," Aaron said. "Your mother will be keeping you busy with your school work and garden and canning work. You need to keep up with your violin lessons also. Once fall arrives, you and Melody will be busy. Don't plan on seeing her every day."

"But Father, we wanted to exchange homes for a month. Melody likes our family so well she would come every day," Miriam protested.

"She might like our family from what she sees when she visits, but her mother needs her just like your mother needs you. There is much to prepare for the winter. The potatoes, squash and carrots and turnips need to be stored in the cellar. Althea Smith told me that she needs help picking apples. We can have two bushels for help with the picking. I will expect you and Anna to talk to her about that."

Lydia took all the girls to the New York store the next day and found some beautiful dresses. Some were not practical in the fancy silks and laces, but she did find a blue pique for Miriam, a flowered pink percale for Anna; Jessie and Emma found matching lavender organdy dresses, and little Tabitha looked so sweet in the ruffled pink organdy. With the girls' dresses purchased, she sat them down with some lemon drops and shopped for herself. At last she was finished. The shoes would have to wait for another day.

"Let's get some groceries and meat at the North Side Market. They have some dried beef that would be good for gravy tonight. Those new 'grables' potatoes that we dug from around the plants would taste delicious with gravy."

During supper, Aaron said, "Since tomorrow is the 4th, I don't have to open the shop. Do you all want to go to the races and ball games tomorrow? We can take a picnic and eat in the park while the band plays. I don't know about staying for the fireworks. It will be so late for the little girls. What do you think, Lydia? Can they take long naps in the morning so they could stay up until after eleven for the fireworks?"

"I think that might work, but I will need help preparing the picnic, along with picking tomatoes and other garden products," Lydia answered. "Can you girls help with the work in the morning so we can go to the races by one?"

"Can I walk to Melody's to see if she will be able to come listen to the band? She could eat with us. I want to tell her about our new dresses," Miriam asked.

"Yes, you may go but don't stay. The little girls need baths, and I must finish canning the corn."

Melody was excited to see Miriam, "Father told me that you were going with us to the fair. What did your mother think about us exchanging homes for a month?"

"Father was the one who said that you probably wouldn't find our family so exciting if you were with us every day," Miriam replied. "He wasn't too much in favor of the idea. But guess what? With the big sale at the New York store, Mother found dresses for all of us to wear to the fair. But what I came here to ask you about is the celebration of the 4th tomorrow. We are taking a picnic to eat in the park while we listen to the band. Would your mother let you eat with us? If Jackson would bring you down to the park, I will save a seat for you."

"I'm going even if Mother says I can't. I'm sick of these four walls," Melody pouted.

"Melody, if your mother says that you can't go, I will stay with you. I will not help you disobey what she thinks is best for your health."

"Let me ask right now so you will know. Mother, can I eat a picnic with the Jensens tomorrow and stay to hear the band? That will get me into fresh air and sunshine," Melody begged.

Mary wheeled her wheelchair into the room, "You could stay for two hours, then you must come home before the night air causes you problems. I will tell Jackson that you will need a ride. Where will you be in the park, Miriam?"

"Probably we will be by the band shell. I don't know for sure, but I will watch for her and save her a seat so she won't have to walk far," Miriam suggested.

Mary returned to the living room, leaving the girls to visit.

"I wish I could visit my aunt in Kansas City before school starts, but I know Father doesn't have any extra money for a train trip just for me," Miriam said sadly. "Besides, he wouldn't let me go alone and Mother can't leave. Sometimes I miss everything we had in Kansas City."

"But I thought you liked this place. Once I am stronger, we could take the train to Kansas City and visit your aunt. I know Father would give me the money if I asked."

"I couldn't ask your father to pay my way. Father and Mother wouldn't let me go even if I did have the money," Miriam complained.

"Leave it to me. I know how to do things like this and your parents will be convinced it is a good idea. If Father was going to send me to Chicago alone on the train, he wouldn't see any problem with you and I going to Kansas City together. Just wait and see." Melody smiled mischievously.

"Melody, I will not go against my parents' wishes, so you can forget any plans about sneaking away," Miriam insisted.

"I said, leave it to me."

"I must go home, Melody. Mother needs my help with the little girls. She is canning corn, which takes so long. We picked three bushels of corn this morning, and by the time we husked it and cut it off the cobs, we only had ten quarts of corn. Sure is a lot of work."

"But it tastes so good," Commented Mary from the sitting room. "I remember my mother canning corn, and it was so good on those cold winter nights. She also had canned beef and pork which we would open when our other meat was used up. It was so much better tasting than anything we could buy. I hope Melody can learn some about canning. Would your mother teach her while she is teaching you, Miriam?"

"Sure, we could put her to work just like the rest of us. It seems like I never have any time to read just for fun any more. Every morning, we are in the garden, or canning, or doing the washing. Would be nice to have a cook and a maid to do all that work."

"No, Miriam, be thankful that you and your mother can do it. I didn't like to do housework when Thomas and I were married, so he hired a cook and Anabell. Later, he hired Jackson to do the yard. After the accident, I couldn't do most of what I had enjoyed before. Now that I have Jesus, I would like to cook for my family and sew. Maybe I could do sewing. I could do that sitting in my chair. Would your mother teach both Melody and me how to sew? I could make clothes for the orphans in Chicago."

Miriam walked home in deep thought. What a change had come in Mary's life. Would Mr. Cramton ever appreciate that change and want to accept Jesus himself? In time, maybe Melody would learn to be honest with her parents. She would keep praying for all three of them. Maybe it would take major trouble to make Mr. Cramton see how desperately he needed God.

CHAPTER ELEVEN

MELODY AND MIRIAM'S ESCAPADE

MELODY HAD RECOVERED from the whooping cough enough to start causing problems for her parents again. One afternoon, Miriam came to visit and found Melody dressed in a beautiful blue lace batiste (summerweight cotton) dress. "Why are you so dressed up, Melody?" Miriam asked dubiously. "Are your parents letting you go to some party or something?"

"We are going to the Ice Cream Palace. I've got a surprise for you," Melody answered.

"We are not going anywhere without asking Mother. Does your mother know you are going out?"

"Oh, she went with Father down to the office. I told her that you were coming over, so she knows I am in good hands," she smiled deceitfully.

"Before we go anywhere, walk with me over to ask Mother. She was in the garden when I left, so we can ask without my little sisters begging to come along. Besides, I need to change this dress. I look like your servant girl," Miriam chuckled.

"Why do you always have to ask your parents? Your mother knows you are with me," Melody asked.

"All the more reason we should tell her where we are going. Who knows, she might need to find me in a hurry. It won't take long to walk over there. Come on," Miriam insisted.

Once they had permission and were walking towards downtown, Melody whispered, "I've figured out a way we can go to Kansas City on the train. Father said that Grandma Cramton wants to visit us, but she is not strong enough to handle walking around on the train. I asked if you and I could go to Kansas City to help her. He wasn't sure, but I kept telling him that the two of us could do anything he could. He is too busy to go anyway, so he agreed, and with a little more pushing, I got him to allow some time to shop in Kansas City."

"You what?" Miriam questioned. "Do you know anything about shopping in Kansas City? I never went without Mother. Who would take us shopping?"

"Don't worry, Grandma knows lots of people. I know she can find someone to take us. Father has already ordered the tickets. Grandma wants to come next Friday so you need to have your clothes ready by then," Melody reported excitedly.

"Wait a minute. I haven't asked Father if I can go, and I only have one dress that would be decent for traveling to Kansas City," Miriam reminded her.

"Let's eat our ice cream fast and go talk to your father. I know I can convince him that Grandma needs our help. You will see I can talk him into it. Hurry up and finish that bite. We've got to run."

"Father doesn't allow us to bother him at work unless it is an emergency," Miriam said.

"Oh poo! I wanted to get this all settled so we can shop for some traveling clothes at the Mercantile. They have some gorgeous dresses with hats to match," Melody bubbled.

"Melody, I can't spend any money for clothes. Father told us this week that until he builds up his business there won't be any extra spending. Besides, Mother bought each of us girls new dresses and made us new calicos (cheap brightly figured cotton) so I don't need any more clothes."

"But we must look our best to go to the city. We are the same size, so why don't you come try on some of my dresses. If you have to pinch pennies, you can use two or three of my dresses. Mother won't mind."

"What if I tore it or stained it while traveling?" Mother would never forgive me for ruining borrowed clothes," Miriam explained.

"Don't worry about that. I have so many I'll never wear them. Now hurry. We can try them on before we meet your father after work." Melody was already paying for the ice cream and walking towards the door.

Running to catch up, Miriam was thinking, "How did I ever get into this? Melody is so determined that I can't stop her. Dear Lord, if You don't want me to go to Kansas City with her, let Father say 'no,'" Miriam prayed.

Back at the Cramton home, Melody pulled out piles of dresses, all colors and styles. Mary, who had returned, called from the sitting room, "Hello girls. Melody, where have you been? I expected you to stay here while I was gone. You didn't tell me you had plans."

"Sorry, Mother, Miriam and I are busy. I'll explain later."

Miriam stopped by Mary's chair and whispered. "Mrs. Cramton, Melody asked me to go to Kansas City with her to bring back her grandmother. Now she wants me to borrow her dresses and we haven't even asked my parents. I can't get her to slow down. Do you approve of this trip? How can I convince her to slow down until I talk to my parents?"

"Miriam, I appreciate your concern. She talked her father into this trip. He was too busy to go for his mother so he was glad to send her. He doesn't realize the problems which could be involved. She can talk her father into anything," Mary said sadly.

"Hurry, Miriam. You need to try on these dresses so we can meet your father in an hour," Melody called from her bedroom.

"Coming, Melody," Miriam called. To Mary she whispered, "Pray that I will know what to do Mrs. Cramton."

"I have been praying, Miriam."

Miriam was shocked to find the pile of dresses Melody had pulled out of her closet. "I only need one dress. These are much too fancy for me."

"Here try on this blue one. You look good in blue." Melody pulled a beautiful taffeta (heavy shiny rayon fabric) with a low neckline, from the pile. "Try it on."

"I can't wear anything with that type of neckline," Miriam protested.

"The boys would really notice you with this dress. You would look like sixteen with it on," Melody promised.

"I'm not trying to get boys to notice me. Father will

help me find the right Christian boy when it is time for me to marry. I will not try on that dress. Haven't you any dresses more my type?" Miriam said firmly.

"Oh, you just don't want to try something exciting. I like making the boys goggle-eyed," Melody chuckled.

"Here is a dress I could wear," Miriam said as she lifted a soft, dark blue velvet with a high lace collar, and lace on the sleeves. "May I try it on?"

"That old thing. I wore it to a party last year. Mother liked it but I never did. You can keep it as far as I am concerned," Melody complained.

"It's beautiful, and it fits me so well. That is all I need. We still have to ask permission from Father, so I will leave it here until we ask him," Miriam remarked.

"Here, try on this mint green. It has the same neckline, so you are well covered if that is what you want. Hurry and try it on so we can run to meet your father," Melody urged.

As they left the bedroom, Miriam stopped to talk to Mary, "Mrs. Cramton, we are going to meet my father after he closes the shop to see what he thinks about this trip. Melody will be home as soon as we talk to him, won't you Melody?" Miriam asked.

Once outside, Melody questioned, "Why did you treat me like a little girl, telling Mother I would be right home? Maybe I have other plans. Now she will expect me home."

"Why shouldn't you go right home? Your father will be coming for the evening meal and you should be there. My father expects me home when the meals are served," Miriam advised.

"Never mind. Let's meet your father so you will know that you are leaving Friday. Let me do all the talking. I know how to handle these things."

Miriam rolled her eyes wondering what Melody would pull on her father to convince him, if he said "no" to her train trip. Melody wasn't used to being told "no," but Miriam knew that if her father said "no," he meant it.

Aaron was walking towards home when the girls ran to meet him. "Oh, Mr. Jensen, I'm so glad to see you," Melody gushed, "I need Miriam's help so badly. Will you let her help me this Friday?"

"What are you talking about Melody? What is happening this Friday?" Aaron asked in irritation.

"Oh, my poor crippled grandmother wants to come visit us, but she can't unless someone helps her riding the train. Father wants me to go but I can't go by myself to Kansas City. He said that if Miriam could go then he was sure we could handle Grandmother. Please, please let Miriam go with me? Poor Grandmother hasn't been out to see our new house. I'm so eager to see her. You will let Miriam go, won't you?" Melody begged.

"Wait a minute. Before I decide anything I need to talk to your father. I will stop by your place after supper tonight," Aaron grumbled while continuing to walk home.

"Oh, he said it was okay. You don't need to talk to him. He really needs us to go," Melody insisted.

"Tell your father that I will be stopping by," Aaron responded sharply. "Come on, Miriam. We need to talk to your mother."

During supper that evening Aaron told Lydia about Melody's request. "I'm not convinced that two young girls should be traveling on the train alone. Melody is so impetuous that no one knows what she might talk Miriam into doing."

"I really would like to go Father. I don't want to stay, but all summer I have missed my friends and Aunt Mable so much. What could happen on the train? Once we are in Kansas City we will be with her grandmother," Miriam begged.

"I know it all sounds good but if her grandmother is so feeble that she needs help to come on the train, how can she do anything with Melody's strong will? I don't feel right about you going, but I will talk to Mr. Cramton tonight since you said that he had purchased the tickets," Aaron sighed.

After her father left, Miriam sat at the table talking with her mother. The little girls had gone outside to play with Anna. "Mother, why doesn't father trust me? I'm old enough to tell Melody 'no' to her scatter-brained ideas."

"We know that you can be trusted Miriam, but Melody insists on pushing adults into her plans. How will you be able to resist without an adult to help you? I would like for you to visit your cousins in Kansas City and Aunt Mable. I know you want to see your friends Mary and Eliza but I'm not sure going with Melody is a wise choice. We will see what your father says when he returns."

After what seemed like hours, Aaron returned looking rather glum. "What did Mr. Cramton say? Can I go? When do we leave?" Miriam begged.

"One question at a time, Miriam. Mr. Cramton was comfortable with the idea of you and Melody going on the train. He said that his mother's carriage and driver would meet you at the train so he felt that you would be in good hands. You may go visit Aunt Mable and your cousins since they live near Mr. Cramton's mother. He said that you will stay overnight and return the next afternoon. He didn't think any problems could happen during that time. I don't think he knows his daughter very well."

"Oh, thank you, Father. I can't wait to see Mary and Eliza!" Miriam squealed.

"Wait a minute. When did I say anything about visiting Mary and Eliza? They don't live near Melody's grandmother."

"But couldn't I call them? Melody said that her grandmother had a telephone now. They could come to see us there. I may not see them for years. Please Father, let me try to call them."

"I don't see that there would be any problem with her calling and inviting them to come to Melody's grandmother's home, Aaron," Lydia suggested.

"Very well, you may call them but if they can not come, you are not to try to visit them. Do you understand?" Aaron said firmly.

"Yes, Father, I will remember. But I will be praying that they can come," Miriam smiled at him.

"You had better be praying for the whole trip, Miriam. I have a feeling you will need God's help to handle Melody. I need to get to bed now. I have a long day tomorrow repairing a plow. Oh, by the way, do you have decent clothes to wear on the train?"

"Melody loaned me a dress, and I have the new one that Mother purchased at the Mercantile sale. That is all I need."

"I suppose you will need some spending money. I have a little put away for emergencies. Ask your mother for it Friday morning," Aaron said as he gave Miriam and Lydia good-night hugs. "See you two in the morning."

Miriam gave her father a big hug. "Oh thank you Father, thank you! On the train coming out here I was determined to go back to Kansas City to live with Aunt Mable this fall, but since then I have learned to love living in a small town. I do miss Mary and Eliza, but not like I did at first."

Friday morning came fast. Miriam had her valise (small overnight bag) packed, her light brown hair freshly curled, and her new dress on, long before Jackson came in the carriage with Melody. "Mother," she begged, "do I look all right? I don't want Melody to be ashamed of me. She always looks so beautiful."

"You look wonderful, Miriam. I'm proud of the way you have learned to do your hair and prepare your clothes. I know Melody doesn't do any of that. The maid does it all for her, so she doesn't appreciate the work that it takes to press her beautiful dresses."

"Here they come," Anna called from the front yard. "You should see Melody. She is gorgeous. She looks like she is sixteen with her hair up."

Miriam looked shocked. "You told me that I couldn't put my hair up until I was sixteen. Why would Melody's mother let her do it now?"

"I don't know Miriam. Probably Melody made such a fuss that Mary just gave in. You know Melody does things like that," Lydia reminded her.

Miriam carried her valise to the porch and waited for

Jackson to come for it. "Come on, Miss Jensen, I will help you into the carriage." Jackson was treating her like a young lady. Miriam felt like a queen going to her first ball.

Melody was so excited that she could hardly sit still. "You will be surprised at all the things I have planned for us," she whispered. "I can't wait to tell you."

"Melody, we will only be in Kansas City twenty-four hours so there won't be time for much extra. I plan to visit my aunt and my cousins and call my two friends from school. By then it will be time to return home."

"Oh, didn't Father tell your father, I had my father buy the tickets for us to return on Monday instead of Saturday," Melody smiled deceptively.

"My parents are expecting me back Saturday evening. How will they know we won't be back until Monday?" Miriam moaned.

"I will tell Jackson to go by the shop and tell your father so they won't worry about you," Melody chuckled.

"Melody, why didn't you tell me this Monday? I don't like you dropping it on me after we leave home."

"Don't you like surprises? We are going to have fun. Just you wait and see," Melody bragged. "I know how to have fun in Kansas City without Grandmother even guessing where we are or what we are doing."

Miriam sent up a silent prayer, "Dear God, help me know what to do. I am afraid Melody will get us into trouble and I can't handle her pushing so hard."

"What's wrong with you, Miriam? You acted like you were praying," Melody said.

"I was, Melody. My father gave me strict instructions to only visit my aunt and my cousins and invite my friends to come to your grandmother's house. That is exactly what I will do. Don't plan on me being involved with any of your plans."

"Party pooper!" Melody whimpered. "I thought you would be glad to get away from this stuffy little town and have some fun."

"I like to have fun. You know that I do, but disobeying my parents is not the right kind of fun."

Melody was pouting, and didn't speak to Miriam again until they were seated on the train. Suddenly she exclaimed, "Look who is getting on the train! There is William and Isaac. Hello, boys. Come over and sit across from us so we will have someone to talk to on this long ride."

Miriam jabbed Melody in the ribs with her elbow. "No, don't invite them over here. I don't want to talk to them all the way to Kansas City."

"Well, I do. You sit over there with Isaac. I'm sitting with William. Come right over here, William," Melody called. Soon she had scooted close and put her hand into his.

Miriam moved over by the window and watched the dry August countryside. Her mood was as dreary as the dry grass and weeds. Father had warned her that Melody might do something unusual, but she would have never guessed this. She felt betrayed. "Once I get to Kansas City, I'm going straight to Aunt Mable's and stay until we leave," she mumbled under her breath.

"What did you say, Miriam?" Isaac moved close and put his arm over her shoulder. "Why don't you relax and enjoy the trip. Quit being so prudish."

Miriam removed Isaac's arm from her shoulder and said, "Isaac, I'm not angry with you. You knew when Melody invited you that our parents would not approve."

"But why should they mind if we travel on the same train to Kansas City?" Isaac asked.

"We are too young to be traveling together. I don't want to do anything to mess up what God has for my life."

"What does God know about what boys and girls do together? He's so far away and so uninterested in what we do. You can't expect Him to be involved," Isaac announced.

"Do you know Jesus personally, Isaac?" Miriam asked, "Because if you did, you would know how very much He loves us and cares about every detail of our life."

Isaac rolled his eyes to the ceiling, "Miriam, I don't know about you. You give up a chance for a good time without your parents knowing what you were doing and say that God is interested in every detail."

"That's not all, Isaac, when I get to Kansas City, I'm going to my Aunt Mable's and stay until we leave," Miriam announced.

"Come on Isaac, let Miriam go to her aunt's," Melody interrupted. "I know of girls in Kansas City who would jump at the chance to go with you. It's time for lunch. Are you coming with us, Miriam?"

"Go on and eat, I have food that Mother prepared for me. As the others left Miriam prayed, "Dear God, what am I going to do? How can I help Melody to understand that this is not the way a child of Your's should act. And that deceiving her parents is a sin, not just mischievous fun. Give me the words to share with her and Isaac and William."

After lunch, Isaac sat by Miriam and asked, "Are you still pouting? Why don't you decide to enjoy the trip? I won't hurt you."

Miriam looked him in the eye and asked, "Are you planning on marrying me?"

"Of course not! Why would you ask such a question? We are only thirteen. I'm not ready to marry anyone," Isaac stated in shock.

"If you are not planning on marrying me, why are you courting me?" Miriam asked pleasantly.

"I'm not courting you. Melody asked if I wanted to go on a fun trip. That is the only reason I am here," Isaac answered.

"If you are not courting me, then we have no business sitting together. If you will excuse me, I see an empty seat over there. That older lady could use some company." Miriam slid past a surprised Isaac and sat by the older lady who smiled graciously at her.

Isaac looked at Melody and rolled his eyes, "You didn't tell me she was so prudish."

Melody smiled and fluttered her eyes, "Come over and sit on the other side of me. I'll find a girl in Kansas City who will enjoy your company. Miriam would just make us all miserable if she went along."

Once the train arrived in Kansas City, Miriam was the first to see Mrs. Cramton's carriage. She could tell it because it looked exactly like Melody's father's carriage. "Here's our ride, Melody. Would it be all right if they left me at Aunt Mable's?"

"Don't you want to meet Grandmother Cramton? She would think you were rude when she probably has a big meal planned for us," Melody said.

"Oh, I should meet her. I can call Aunt Mable from there," Miriam smiled.

Mrs. Cramton was indeed glad to see the girls. She took one look at Isaac and William and said in strict tones, "What, may I ask, are you young men doing here? I was told by Melody's father that she and Miriam were staying with me. You may eat with us but we will find a place for you at the hotel right after the meal. You girls may go upstairs to wash up, and you boys may go to the servants washroom. Dinner will be served in the dining room in ten minutes. You boys follow me." She left at a fast trot with the boys hurrying to keep up.

"Melody, you said that your grandmother wasn't able to walk without help. Wasn't that the reason that we came to Kansas City?" Miriam asked cautiously.

"Oh, well, she has her good days and bad days. This must be one of the good ones," Melody chirped as she skipped up the steps. Miriam could tell that Melody didn't want to talk about it.

Back in the dining room, Mrs. Cramton had Isaac and William sitting stiffly on the fancy chairs, with their hair combed properly. Miriam could see that she was going to love Mrs. Cramton. No one pulled any mischief around her.

"Mrs. Cramton, could I call my Aunt Mable from here? She doesn't know I'm in town and I wish to visit their home while I am here," Miriam asked.

"Miss Jensen, you are welcome to stay with me. I've made arrangements for those two whippersnappers at the hotel so you would be perfectly safe staying here, but I know you wish to see your aunt. The phone is here in the hall," Mrs. Cramton announced.

"Thank you for offering me a room, Mrs. Cramton. I haven't seen my aunt for months and it will probably be a year before our family can come for a visit. But I would love to sit with you on the train on the way back."

"We will do just that, young lady," Mrs. Cramton said as she bustled off to check on dinner.

Miriam held her breath as she gave the operator her aunt's number. "Oh please let her be home. I don't want to stay here with Melody." It was a relief when her aunt answered.

"Oh, Miriam, where are you? You sound so close. Are you here in town? Can you come visit us?" Aunt Mable gushed.

"Yes, Aunt Mable, I am here at Mrs. Cramton's home. My friend, Melody Cramton, and I arrived this afternoon, and will be leaving with Mrs. Cramton Monday. May I stay with you until then?" Miriam asked.

"Yes, Uncle Charles will be over to pick you up right away. I can't wait to hear all about your family."

"No, don't come yet. Mrs. Cramton has dinner all prepared. Have Uncle Charles wait to come until after dinner," Miriam suggested.

Miriam hung up the phone with relief. That part of her problem was settled.

In spite of herself, Miriam enjoyed the formal dinner with Grandmother Cramton. She was a witty conversationalist. Even Isaac and William relaxed and laughed at her humorous stories. As the maid passed the roasted chicken and creamed corn along with fresh garden tomatoes, they all had some good laughs. Mrs. Cramton told stories of her childhood. "When I was your age, my parents would never have allowed me to ride on a train with a young man, without an adult chaperon. Melody, do your parents allow you to bring young men along on your travels?"

Melody's face turned bright red and she said quietly, "No, Grandmother. They didn't know that Isaac and William were coming on the trip. Please don't tell them," she begged.

"We will have to see about that young lady. We will talk about it later. Now, young ladies and young men, what would you like for dessert? We have vanilla custard or strawberry ice cream," Mrs. Cramton announced.

After each had chosen their dessert, Mrs. Cramton looked at Melody. "What are your plans for tomorrow, Melody?"

"I told Isaac and William that we could go to the horse race tomorrow. I have a little money to place some bets."

"Melody Cramton, I'm ashamed of you! My granddaughter gambling! I will let you go watch the races since you promised these young men but no betting on the races."

They were finishing up their dessert when the butler announced that someone was at the door. "That must be Uncle Charles," Miriam announced. "Aunt Mable said he would come for me after dinner. Thank you so much for the wonderful dinner, Mrs. Cramton. If you will excuse me, I will get my valise and go with Uncle Charles," Miriam said.

Uncle Charles carried her valise and helped her into the carriage, "Oh, Uncle Charles, it is so good to see you. It seems like years since we left Kansas City."

"You've grown up since you left last spring. You've become a beautiful young lady. Your cousins, Elizabeth and Suzanne, can't wait until you arrive. They will probably talk you to death tonight," Uncle Charles laughed.

Miriam hadn't realized how much she missed her aunt and uncle until now. Once in the house, she asked, "Aunt Mable, do you think I could invite my best friends, Mary and Eliza over to visit tomorrow? It would be wonderful if I could visit them a short time."

"Yes, we can call them in the morning. Maybe they would like to come for lunch. Sometime while you are here I would like to take you shopping, to help me purchase Christmas presents for your family. Would you be willing to take the time to do that? That way, I could send them with you when you return, and I wouldn't have to ship them."

"Yes, I would love to shop with you. I know what Anna wants, and could probably help with some ideas for the other girls. It might be more difficult to find something for Father, but I know that Mother needs some material to make baby clothes."

"What! Is your mother going to have a baby? She didn't tell me that in her last letter," Aunt Mable said in surprise.

"She hasn't told anyone except Father and me. She knows that everyone will think that five girls is enough. The baby isn't due until late winter, so she won't tell until later," Miriam smiled.

CHAPTER TWELVE

KANSAS CITY AND THE TRIP HOME

S ATURDAY DAWNED bright and sunny as Aunt Mable gathered the family for an early breakfast. "If we are going to do all the Christmas shopping for Miriam's family, we have to have an early start. Charles, can you deliver us downtown as soon as we are ready? It will probably take most of the day, so we will eat at that nice little restaurant at noon. You can pick us up around three; we either will be done or too tired to shop further," she laughed.

"Aunt Mable, you are so nice," Miriam stated softly. "I thought I was only coming to bring Melody's grandmother to Beloit. I didn't expect to visit you, much less go shopping and have a visit with my friends. Oh thank you, thank you," Miriam reached over to give her aunt a hug.

"This is saving me time and shipping expense, Miriam, if you help me pick out the Christmas gifts and take them back with you," her aunt replied.

Once at the largest store in the city, Miriam guided her aunt in choices of clothing for each of her sisters, and some warm mittens for everyone. "Why don't you, Elizabeth and Suzanne go to the soda fountain for a soda while I purchase your gift. That will finish almost all of our gifts."

Aunt Mable returned with a huge smile, "I found the most perfect gift for you, Miriam. You are in for a wonderful surprise. If you girls are finished with your drinks, let's walk down to the little restaurant for an early lunch."

On the way to lunch they saw a poster which announced: "William Allen White to speak here Saturday afternoon at two p.m. The community is invited to hear the new editor of the Emporia Gazette."

"Look, Aunt Mable, I wish Melody could hear him. Her father speaks highly of Mr. White and his colorful editorials. Could we stay to here him? Maybe I can learn something to tell Mr. Cramton," Miriam requested.

"Should we try to call Melody's grandmother to see if Melody will be home for lunch? Maybe she and the boys could join us," Aunt Mable suggested.

"I'm sure if they went to horse races, they will be gone all day. Melody sounded like she didn't intend to come back where her grandmother could complain about her actions. But we can try."

They did call Rosie Cramton but she responded with, "I know she would love to hear Mr. White because her father speaks of him often, but, unfortunately, she will not return until late afternoon."

After lunch, they entered the quiet theater early, to sit in front row seats. Aunt Mable had read some about Mr. White. "I read that he had to borrow $3000 to buy the Gazette, yet he lives in a fancy house with a stairway designed by Frank Lloyd Wright, the famous architect. The Populist party gives him 'fits' because of his promotion of the Republican party."

Wearing a white suit and a gaudy tie, the chubby William Allen White walked out onto the stage. Miriam found it difficult to believe he was only 28 years old. He started his strong pronouncements of what was wrong with Kansas. She knew she would never forget his passionate statements on the condition of the state government. He called them shabby, wild-eyed, rattle-brained fanatics, and said, "the Populist influence has made the citizenry meaner than a spavined, distempered mule."

"I wish Melody's father could have heard that speech. He likes editors who are outspoken in their beliefs," Miriam spoke in awe, as they walked back to the store after the speech.

Sunday was cool and cloudy, with the threat of rain, as Miriam dressed to go to church with her aunt and uncle. "Aunt Mable, will you help me with this dress of Melody's? I can't get it pressed after being rumpled in the valise."

"That is beautiful material, Miriam. And blue looks so good on you."

"It's too fancy for most places I go in Beloit. The girls at church don't wear dresses like this except for Melody. Melody insisted that I take it to wear in Kansas City. She has closets full of dresses prettier than this but she doesn't appreciate them. She wants dresses like mine so she can help us with baking and washing. She constantly surprises me with what she chooses to do."

The cool damp weather couldn't dampen Miriam's excitement. She was thinking, "I get to go back to our church and see all my friends." She slipped into the beautiful blue velvet with the lace collar and cuffs. "I wish I was old enough to put my hair up, but this bow will match my dress."

As she came down the stairs, Uncle Charles exclaimed, "My! You look very grown up, Miriam. That dress is very flattering with your blue eyes."

Miriam felt her face turn red. "Thank you, Uncle Charles. My friend loaned me the dress. She wanted me to look extra nice for the trip."

"I can't wait to see Mary and Eliza; It seems like years since I've seen them," she bubbled with excitement as they rode to church.

Eliza was waiting on the church steps when the carriage came to a stop by the church. She looked much older than Miriam remembered her. Miriam almost jumped from the carriage before her uncle stopped. Once on the ground, she ran to give Eliza a big hug. "It's so good to see you. It will take hours to tell you about life in Beloit."

"You sound excited about it. Before you left you were so sure it would be dull," Eliza reminded her. "Mary is in class waiting for us, so wait to tell us both later."

"You won't believe all that has happened to me," Miriam answered.

Following church, Eliza and Mary joined the family for a delicious lunch. After lunch the girls came into the kitchen to help Aunt Mable with the dishes. "It is wonderful to have five girls doing dishes. I can retire from dish washing," she said laughingly.

"This is fun, Aunt Mable. At home, Anna and I do most of the housework, because Jesse is usually keeping

Emma and Tabitha occupied so Mother can sew or work in the garden."

"I suppose you girls also know how to bake bread and pies?" Aunt Mable questioned.

"Oh, yes. Mother taught us that before we left here. Now we do most of the cooking every day," Miriam answered.

Once the dishes were done, the girls sat on the porch swings and requested that Miriam tell them all about her exciting life in Beloit.

"Did you really see Indians and have a tornado go right through town?" Elizabeth asked.

"Not only did the tornado go through town, but it destroyed houses and our neighbor's barn, and all the men came to rebuild it. After it was rebuilt, he invited everyone in town to come for a supper and barn dance," Miriam announced.

"Did your father let you go?" asked Mary. "I didn't think your family went to dances when you lived here."

"In Beloit everyone goes to the square dances and box suppers. I didn't see anyone drinking and they asked Father to play with the other fiddlers," Miriam answered.

The afternoon went much too fast. Eliza's father came for the girls. As they said goodbye to Miriam, Mary said, "I can't believe your life is so exciting. Wish we could move to Beloit."

Miriam sat alone on the swing thinking, "And to think, I was convinced that I would hate living in a small town, and now my friends want to move there."

The next morning, Aunt Mable called early, "You need to get up and pack, Miriam. We need to take you and all your packages to Mrs. Cramton's right after lunch. And I want to save some time for just the two of us to visit before you go."

They piled everything near the front door. "Now let's sit in the parlor for a visit. Elizabeth and Suzanne said they wanted to fix lunch as a special treat before you leave," Aunt Mable announced.

"Do you think you can visit us, Aunt Mable? I know with the baby due in February, we won't be traveling for ages and ages."

"I've been talking to your uncle, and he mentioned that it was a possibility next spring before the weather turns hot. I hear that the hot winds out on the prairie make it seem so much hotter," Aunt Mable answered.

Elizabeth came to the door, "Mother, we don't know how to fry eggs. Will you come help?"

Following lunch, Uncle Charles delivered Miriam to Mrs. Cramton's home. Mrs. Cramton looked flustered, "I'm glad you are here Miss Jensen. My granddaughter is refusing to pack. Says she is going to call her father to allow her to stay with her friends another week. I told her that we are all leaving today and that was that, but she has not packed."

Miriam walked up the long flight of stairs to Melody's room. Melody was sitting on the bed pouting. "My grand-mother told Father about Isaac and William coming with us, and I know if I go home, I will be in trouble. I'm going to stay here until Father cools off," she announced boldly.

"Melody, I think you have pushed your father too far this time. You have to go home now and face the consequences. It won't be any easier if you wait a week. Here, let me help you pack. We have to leave in thirty minutes. Isaac and William are here, and the rest of us are ready to leave."

Melody half-heartedly started throwing her dresses in the valise. "I didn't get to go shopping or even go downtown or see any friends except Anita. It's just not fair."

"You remember, don't you, that the reason we came to Kansas City was to bring your crippled grandmother to Beloit. We have been able to stay an extra two days, so let's go home. Waiting won't make it any better."

Melody stomped down the stairs, leaving Miriam to carry her valise. Mrs. Cramton looked at her granddaughter and announced, "Young lady, you carry your own valise. Miriam has enough to carry without carrying yours."

Melody stomped on outside carrying her valise. Mrs. Cramton whispered to Miriam, "Would you care to sit with me on the ride home, Miss Jensen? I know Melody will sit with those young whippersnappers. Even though I don't approve, I will leave it to her father to straighten out that situation."

"Yes, Mrs. Cramton, I would love to sit with you," Miriam answered.

The train was pulling into the station as they arrived. Melody marched into their car with Isaac and William following like obedient little lambs. They wanted no business of arguing with her grandmother.

Mrs. Cramton chuckled, "Scared those two boys, I did. I told them after you left Friday night, that I wanted no funny business from them, or I would put them on the first train home. They have been very quiet and obedient since, although I can't say the same for my granddaughter. I can not believe her father has allowed her to get so out of hand. Were you aware that she was spending time with these boys?"

The train was starting to move as Miriam thought through the answer. "Melody is my friend, Mrs. Cramton. In fact she has been my only friend since we arrived in Beloit and I know she is lonesome with no brothers or sisters, so sometimes I didn't say anything when she would take me to the Ice Cream Palace to meet them. I enjoyed the time also, so I told her I would only go if we would tell her mother and mine where we were going. We didn't tell them that Isaac and William would be there also. I feel bad about that because my father is very protective of me. He wants to help me find just the right Christian husband and he would not approve of me seeing Isaac and William every week. Neither of them goes to church, so I'm almost sure they aren't Christians."

"Thank you for being honest with me, Miriam. That makes me feel better knowing that you were encouraging Melody to tell her mother where you were going. They have trusted her too much. But let's change the subject. Tell me about your family. Melody said that you have four sisters. That must keep your mother very busy."

"Yes, she is, and so are Anna and I because we do most of the cooking. Did you know that Melody came to learn how to bake bread, and she has helped us with the washing? She said that no one had taught her to do that at home. I guess she has too much time on her hands and thinks of mischief or something because she is bored to tears. I never have enough time with four sisters."

"I will have to talk to Mary about requiring Melody to learn some cooking and to help with the housework. With Mary in the wheelchair, Melody should be doing more. Besides, at thirteen, she needs to know how to cook and bake a pie. She might marry some young man in a few years and not even know how to boil water. I remember before I married, my mother made me learn everything. She said she didn't want to hear from her son-in-law that I had burned his steak," Mrs. Cramton chuckled.

"You remind me of my great grandmother, Mrs. Cramton. I still miss her. She took in my mother and her father when her mother died. She died several years ago," Melody said quietly.

"Mr. Cramton died ten years ago. It seems like yesterday. He was a traveling evangelist, bringing tent revivals all over the East. I went with him after our son was raised."

"Your husband was a Christian?" Miriam asked in disbelief. "Melody's father doesn't seem to have any interest in being a Christian. He seems to be unhappy about Mary and Melody believing in Jesus. Why is that?"

"Our son resented his father being gone so often, that he refused to accept Jesus. Sometimes I think we made a mistake of not making his salvation more important than evangelizing other people. Mr. Cramton would receive so many calls to bring revivals into so many cities, that he couldn't take them all, but even with the ones he did take, he was gone too much, and Thomas resented that. He seemed to think that God was responsible for his father being gone. I keep praying that he will understand that he needs Christ just like the rest of us," Mrs. Cramton answered sadly.

"We've been praying for him also, Mrs. Cramton." They were both sitting quietly, thinking, when Miriam overheard Melody talking to Isaac and William.

"When we get home, I will find a girl for you, Isaac, who will not be such a prude. I know of some great places to go. Father gives me money each week to spend as I like, so we can have fun without Miriam."

Miriam couldn't believe her ears. "Melody never seems to learn. O Lord," she prayed, "help her see that as Your child she is not only disobeying her parents, but making You very sad."

"Look!" Melody called. "We are almost home. I'm tired of this noisy old train."

"She's wanting to be home now? That granddaughter of mine is never satisfied. I hope Thomas will see that he has to lay down the law with her before it is too late," Mrs. Cramton said quietly.

"I'm thankful to be home too, Mrs. Cramton, but not for the same reason. I miss my family. We may have some arguments but we have some fun times together," Miriam said.

"Will you come visit me, young lady? Besides Thomas' family, you are the only person I know in town," Mrs. Cramton asked.

"Oh, yes, Mrs. Cramton. I will visit, and so will my mother. She knows several older women in town who might visit with you, and there are several older ladies in our church. Could we adopt you as our substitute grandmother?"

"I would love that. It would be wonderful to have five more grandchildren," Mrs. Cramton smiled.

Jackson was waiting with the carriage when they arrived. Melody whispered to Isaac and William, "Wait here on the train until we are gone. I don't want Jackson to see you." They nodded in agreement.

Jackson loaded all their valises and packages in the carriage and helped the women into the carriage. "We are all set, Jackson. Take Miriam to her home first," Melody demanded.

Jessie was the first to see Miriam arrive, and ran to tell her mother, "Mother, Mother, Miriam is home, and she has a bunch of packages."

Lydia came to the door, and Miriam called to her, "Come meet Mrs. Cramton, Mother, while Jackson unloads all my packages."

"I'm so glad to meet you, Mrs. Cramton. Mary has become a very special friend to me. I hope that you will enjoy your visit here."

"I know that I will. Your daughter has made my trip here very enjoyable, and I hope to be seeing more of her and your family. Mary wrote that you had been a wonderful friend," Mrs. Cramton said.

Miriam was surrounded by her sisters with questions as she tried to change into her workday dress. "Give me a few minutes, and I will tell you everything," she requested.

"Did you see Aunt Mable? Did you see our cousins Elizabeth and Suzanne? Did you visit our old church? What did you eat, and what is in all those packages? Are they for us? Can we open them now?"

"One question at a time. Yes, I stayed with Aunt Mable and Uncle Charles and had good time with Elizabeth and Suzanne. I told them all about you, and life in Beloit. They want to come visit us next spring. The packages are from Aunt Mable for Christmas, and no, you can't open them now. But I did get some candy for each of you. Now may I sit down for a minute? I'm tired from the long trip," Miriam said.

Following supper, Miriam shared more about her trip. "Sounds like our prayers for you were answered," Aaron said. "After Jackson came by the shop to say that you were staying an extra two days, I was concerned about Melody. I can see that I had reason to be. You handled it very well, Miriam. I am proud of you."

Miriam smiled at her father's praise. "Thank you Father. I kept praying that I would know what to do. I felt like coming right back home when I found that Melody had paid for William and Isaac to come. Grandmother Cramton is going to talk to her son about Melody. I am afraid it will not be a happy time tonight."

"You look tired, Miriam. Would you like to go to bed early? Tomorrow is wash day, so I will need your help early," Lydia remarked.

"Yes, Mother, I am tired. It will be so good to be in my own bed. Aunt Mable was so nice to me, and we had a good visit, but I am thankful to be home. As much as I hate doing the washing, it will seem good to be back in my own family."

As she drifted off to sleep, Miriam prayed, "Dear Lord, I know that Melody probably didn't have a happy time tonight with her parents. Help her to learn that disobedience leads to some unhappy consequences."

The next morning dawned bright and sunny as Miriam and her mother started the washing. Father had pumped the wash water and had it heating on the old stove in the washhouse. "Call Anna to fix breakfast for us while we get the white clothes washed. You can run them through the wringer while I wash them," Lydia requested.

By noon Lydia announced, "That's all of the washing. Dump the rinse water on the flower beds and let's eat a bowl of beans. I am ready for some food and rest."

"May I take Melody's dress back to her this afternoon? I can iron it after dinner," Miriam asked.

"Yes, you may take it back, and take some of the cookies to the Cramtons," Lydia suggested.

"Why don't you go with me, Mother? We can go after Father gets home from the shop. I know that Grandmother Cramton wants to visit with you." Lydia agreed to go with her.

The minute Jackson opened the door to their knock, Miriam could see that it was not a happy place. Not seeing Melody anywhere, she blurted out, "I came to bring Melody's dress back. Is she here?"

"Yes, she is in her bedroom," Mary answered. "I know that she wants to talk to you."

Miriam left her mother visiting with Mary and Grandmother Cramton.

"Melody, are you in here?" she called from the doorway. At last she saw Melody curled up on the bed crying.

"Do you want to talk, Melody? Can I help?" Miriam asked.

"No one can help. I am a prisoner in my own home. Father was so angry when he met us at the door last night. I have never seen him get so upset. His face turned beet red and he said I was not to leave this house for a month, and that I would be tutored at home for this whole school year. I told him that I wouldn't disobey him again, but he said that he can't trust me anymore. It's terrible. He's so unfair. Just because I paid for Isaac and William to come with us. I wish I could run away and never come back. That would teach him. He hates me, or he wouldn't be so cruel," Melody sobbed.

Miriam sat down beside Melody and put her arm around her. "Do you really think he hates you? Could it be that he loves you so much that he wants to protect you?"

"No, I'm old enough to do as I wish. He has always let me do as I wished before," Melody rationalized.

"Well, we are the same age and I know that I am not old enough to make all my own decisions. Mother and Father see problems that I never see because they have learned from hard lessons. Because they love me, they have to say 'no' to some of my ideas. But as they see me making right choices, they are allowing me to make more of my own decisions. I may not like them to tell me 'no,' but I know that they want what is best for me."

"But your parents are Christians and my father isn't. I have never seen your father get as angry as Father did last night. I thought he was going to have a heart attack or something. Mother had to calm him down, or I think he would have hit me. It scared me to see him so angry."

"Is your mother going to be teaching you this year, or is your father going to hire a tutor?" Miriam asked.

"I told him if I couldn't go to school with my friends, I wanted to study with you, but he said that my mother would be doing the teaching. I asked about my music lessons and how I could keep up with the orchestra, which

148

he thinks is so important. He said that he would hire a tutor to come each day to give me lessons. He absolutely will not allow me to leave home unless he or Mother is with me. How can they be so terrible?" Melody pouted.

"I suppose that means that we are not going to the Kansas State Fair next month," Miriam said hesitantly.

"He said that we would go since he had already purchased the tickets for our families, and he doesn't want to disappoint your family. But he won't let me ride any carnival rides or do anything except stay right with him and Mother. That will be so dull. Wish I could stay home, but he absolutely wouldn't allow that," Melody related.

"You might find that you enjoy studying at home, Melody. Even with all the distractions of my little sisters, I find that I have all my studies done in the morning, so that in the afternoon we can cook or sew. I've learned to cook several new foods and help mother can vegetables. She has taught me to knit and crochet. And, some afternoons, I can curl up with a good book while the little girls are asleep. That is much easier than spending all day in school with some classmates who don't want to study and like to cause problems."

"Don't you miss spending time with other girls? I don't think I can stand it being home with Mother all day. I won't get to see Isaac and William, and the girls in my class probably won't come see me. They will think I've got some terrible disease, being required to stay at home all the time," Melody moaned.

While they were talking, Grandmother Cramton walked into the room, "Oh, there you are Melody. I've been looking for you. Your mother needs some clothes from their bedroom. Lydia said that she would do some altering on them. Would you find them? It's the maid's day off. She said you would know where they were in her closet."

"Do I have to? Miriam and I are visiting," Melody protested.

"It won't take long," her grandmother answered.

"How long are you planning to stay, Mrs. Cramton?" Miriam asked.

"I plan to be going home next week. Mary needs to start Melody's schooling. She doesn't need me underfoot during that time. I imagine she will have some difficulties with Melody's attitude and may have to crack the whip. It would be better if I wasn't here to interfere. They may have some battles until Melody gets the message that her parents love her enough to mean business. They have waited almost too long to start showing her they love her enough to say 'no,'" Mrs. Cramton announced.

"I know Melody is going to argue with her mother. She argues with me. I just hope that she doesn't get into a real battle with her mother. They need to work together so that your son will come to know the Christ that they know. Their fighting will just make him more angry at them and God."

"You seem to understand my son quite well, Miriam. That is exactly what he would do. He will blame God for making his home so miserable. He blamed God for his father being gone so much, and for the difficult time we had when their wasn't much money. He said that if God really loved us He would have his father stay home and make a decent living. That is why he wants to make lots of money. He thinks it will bring him happiness. I think he is beginning to see that it hasn't."

Walking home from the Cramtons, Lydia said, "Mary told me that she was going to be teaching Melody at home. She told me that she was afraid Melody would not listen to her because she is already so angry at not being allowed to go anywhere with her friends. I wish there was some way that we could help."

"Mother, Melody is so angry that she may run away so that no one can find her. She told me that she thinks her father hates her. I tried to make her see that he is making her stay home because he loves her. I don't think that she believed me. What more can we do? She wants you to teach her, but her father said that her mother would do the teaching except for music," Miriam said quietly.

Miriam and Anna started their studies that week, so Miriam was too busy for a few days to visit Melody. "Maybe she is working well with her mother after all," she reasoned.

One morning, they were deep into a reading lesson from the Bible when someone pounded on the door. Lydia opened it to find Jackson. "Here is a note from Mrs. Cramton. She wanted me to bring you over right away. She said that it was urgent."

After reading the note, Lydia instructed, "Miriam, can you take care of things here, and Anna will you start dinner? I should be back by noon."

Jackson let Lydia off at the front door, and Mary was waiting at the door before she knocked. "Thank heavens you have come, Lydia. I'm beside myself with frustration. Melody just will not do her studies. She keeps telling me that she is in prison and that we hate her. No amount of talking, praying or demanding will convince her to do her work. Just before you came, she ran into her room, slammed the door and locked it. Did we make a mistake by not allowing her to go to school?" Mary sobbed.

Putting her arms around Mary, Lydia answered, "No, Mary, you didn't make a mistake, but since Melody doesn't know the meaning of 'no,' it will be difficult for awhile. Can I talk to her?"

Just at that moment, the door burst open. Jackson had a screaming, yelling Melody by the arm. "Mrs. Cramton, I was putting the horse away when I saw Melody climbing out of her window with her valise. I knew that Mr. Cramton said she was not to leave the house. What do you wish for me to do with her?" Jackson asked breathlessly.

"Let go of me!" she yelled shaking his hand loose. "If you hadn't seen me, I would have been on the next train out of here. I hate this place. You all hate me and make me feel miserable. I'm going to go to Chicago where I can do what I want. You can't force me to stay here."

"Sit down, Melody," Lydia demanded. "You are not going to do any such thing." She noticed that Melody was dressed in a very low-necked dress, and had her hair pulled up. She prayed silently for the right words.

"Melody, you want your parents to give you freedom and to treat you like an adult? Why are you acting like a naughty child by sneaking out the window dressed like a harlot?"

Melody looked up in shock, "I am not a harlet! This dress makes me look older so I could travel without anyone asking questions."

"If you want to be treated like an adult you will have to act like one. The longer you rebel, the longer it will be before you are given any freedom. You have to make the choice, Melody. You can act like a spoiled brat, and make yourself and everyone else miserable, or choose to obey your parents, study with your mother, and, in time, be given some freedom. You are correct about noone being able to force you to willingly obey. But, in disobeying your parents, you are also rebelling against God, who loves you even more than your parents do. He has a wonderful plan for your life, but He will only show it to you as you choose to obey His rules and commands," Lydia entreated.

"But how is God going to show me His plan? Does He write it in the sky or write me a letter?" Melody asked stubbornly.

"He has sent you a letter, Melody. You already have it," Lydia stated.

"I do? Oh, you mean the Bible. I haven't seen anything in there about what I am to do with my life, or who I should marry. In fact, the Bible seems to me a book of boring stories. How can there be anything about me in it?" Melody asked.

"Would you like an assignment for your grammar lesson? Read Genesis 37–47 with your mother this week, and find out about a boy who could have thought his family and God were terrible to him. You might learn something about how God reveals His plan to people. It is one of Miriam's favorite stories."

"Could I come study with you and Miriam and Anna?" Melody asked.

"Your parents have decided that you should study

with your mother. So that is what you should do. Maybe after you prove that you are willing to do that, we might be able to work out some other types of studies. Your mother and I have talked some about sharing teaching. She knows so much about horse riding, which our girls wish to learn, and I could teach you to bake bread and pies. How does that sound to you?" Lydia asked.

"I guess I could try. I know I won't like studying here at home, but I will try," Melody said sullenly.

Mary smiled thankfully at Lydia, "You must get back to your family."

As she let herself out the door, Lydia looked back at Melody, "I'll be back next week," she called. "You can tell me what you have learned from Genesis then."

CHAPTER THIRTEEN

MR. CRAMTON AND THE KANSAS STATE FAIR

MIRIAM WAS SO BUSY with her own studies that she almost forgot about Melody's problems. Lydia said early Wednesday morning, "Girls, the Kansas State fair is in three weeks. We have garden produce to preserve, and your studies to work on, so our days will be full. Can I count on you to work hard and help me?"

"Yes, Mother," Miriam answered. "I can help with the canning, if Anna can take care of the daily cooking."

"But I have to cook all the time!" Anna complained. "Couldn't we trade off? Canning is more fun than cooking three meals a day. Let Miriam do that. I want to work with you, Mother."

"Let's not fight. Miriam will help me preserve the food one day, and the next day you may help, Anna. How does that sound?" Lydia asked.

"That is much better. Sometimes I wish I was Melody

and did not have to do any of this hard work. She just has her studies and that is all she has to do. Wouldn't that be nice?" Anna said wistfully.

"We need to visit Melody this week. I told her that I would be back. We must hurry through our work and studies so we can visit there this afternoon." Lydia announced.

"We will work fast, Mother," Miriam and Anna said together.

"Don't we get to play this morning?" Jessie asked.

"I need you to help me pick and snap beans, Jessie. Emma and Tabitha can play in the dirt by the garden while we pick. Let's stop right now, and ask God to help Melody work hard on her studies today also," Lydia suggested.

Lydia and the girls made fast progress on the garden produce. Anna read stories to Emma and Tabitha so they would stay on their beds to take naps after dinner. Once the girls were awake, Lydia called Miriam and Anna from their reading, "Let's walk over to see Melody and Mary. It is a beautiful day outside."

Miriam carried Tabitha, and Lydia took Emma by the hand. It was a wonderful Indian summer day — one of the last of the beautiful days before winter hits — with the trees beginning to turn red and gold. The sounds of quail, with their calls of "bob-white!" came from the dried weeds near the road. "I love the sound of those little birdies," Jessie exclaimed.

"I wish it would stay this way all year," Anna commented. "I don't like the cold and snow when we have to stay inside all day."

"But if we didn't have any changes we wouldn't appreciate days like this, Anna," her mother remarked.

Melody and Mary were out in the flower garden terrace when the Jensen girls came walking up the lane. "Come out here and join us," Mary called when she heard them.

"Melody had all her lessons done before noon, except for piano and violin which will be later this afternoon. It is too nice to stay inside. What brings you all out today? I thought you were busy preserving your garden produce," Mary asked.

"The girls helped so well and we needed a break. We wanted to visit with you," Lydia answered.

Melody said, "I can't wait until we go to the fair. Father said that William Jennings Bryant will be speaking, and he wants to interview him. They also will have balloon rides, and a circus, and races. I've never seen any of that. Maybe, by that time, Father will let me go on some rides."

"Don't count on that, Melody. Your Father and I have agreed that you must stay with us at all times."

"You mean I can't go on any rides? What is the use of going if I can't enjoy any of it? I don't want to sit all day listening to speakers," Melody complained.

"Your father hasn't been feeling well lately, so don't push him. He doesn't act like he enjoys anything right now. I've been praying all the time for him, but God doesn't seem to be changing him."

"But Mother, didn't you tell me that God doesn't force anyone? He gives everyone the choice to either obey or disobey Him. I wish God would hurry up too, Father is no fun to be around any more."

The next weeks flew by. Melody was allowed to come often to help with the garden and canning. Sometimes

Jackson delivered Mary to help Lydia with the preparing of the vegetables for canning. "That's something I can do sitting down, and you teach me so much. Some day, Melody and I might get brave and convince the cook to let us can our vegetables. It's a shame to throw so much away. Most of our neighbors have their own gardens and orchards."

"It does make it more enjoyable to have you here, Mary. You are doing so well in your Bible lessons, you soon may be teaching me."

Mary laughed, "It is difficult to study when Thomas is home. At first he didn't seem to mind me reading the Bible, but now he complains if he sees me reading it. He keeps saying he is going on that tour to look for a place to move and start a new newspaper. He acts like he wants to escape from something."

"Could it be that he is running from God?" Lydia asked. "Without the hope of believing Christ died for him, nothing will make him happy or satisfied."

"I'm sure that is most of the problem, although he hasn't looked well lately. He is short of breath when he walks, but he will not go see the doctor. He tells me he is healthy and doesn't want any old doctor poking on him," Mary said sadly. "So I don't mention it. I just pray for him."

"That's the most important thing you can do, Mary. God can reach into peoples lives where we can't. You can be sure that our family has been praying. Do you think that he will still go to the Kansas Fair? That date is coming up soon. Aaron and I are looking forward to that. We haven't had a family vacation for ages."

"Oh, he will go because he planned it, but I am afraid

he might ruin it for the rest of us with his grumpy attitude," Mary answered.

The day before the fair started, Thomas dropped by the shop to remind Aaron, "Is your family still planning to go with us to the fair? The train leaves at 9 o'clock tomorrow. Shall I have Jackson stop by for your family and trunks? We will be going right by your lane."

"That would help so that I don't have to harness up old Bessie and Joe and bring them back before we leave." Aaron answered.

Bright and early the next morning, Jackson arrived with the Cramton's carriage. He helped Aaron load the trunks, and seated Lydia and the girls in the back seat. Thomas and Aaron walked behind the carriage to the station. "There's the train. I can hear the whistle from here." Thomas said.

As they rode in the carriage, Mary whispered to Lydia, "Thomas is in a good mood today. Melody and I prayed together last night that he wouldn't ruin the trip for everyone."

Lydia smiled, "We will keep praying for him today. Maybe something on this trip will open his eyes to what he is missing."

On the train, Melody and Miriam were carrying on a long conversation about school and their violin lessons. "I just wish Father would let your father give me violin lessons. That stuffy old music teacher from school makes me learn every note until I am sick of playing the same note over and over," Melody complained. "Your father just has me listen to him play and to play what I hear."

At noon, Thomas took them to the buffet car for dinner. Lydia had packed some apples and dried fruit in case they didn't have food on the train, but she was thankful for the meal. She could save the fruit for later.

Once in Wichita, Thomas hired a carriage to deliver them to the hotel. "As soon as you are ready, we can walk to the platform where William Jennings Bryant will be speaking. After that, the circus performs, which I am sure the children will enjoy."

As Senator Bryan was speaking, the girls became bored. Melody whispered to Miriam, "He may be a great senator in Father's eyes but this is dull. I wish there was something else we could do."

They whispered a few more minutes and quietly left their seats and walked out. "Let's walk through the carnival. It is right close. No one will miss us for a few minutes," Miriam suggested.

An hour later, Thomas was able to interview the senator for a few minutes for the paper. "Now, children, off to the circus," he announced. "It is in the big tent over there. Come, and I will purchase tickets for everyone. Where are Melody and Miriam?"

"I don't know," Aaron answered. "They were sitting behind us when Senator Bryant started speaking. It isn't like Miriam to leave without telling us. Did she say anything to you, Lydia?"

"No, Aaron. Surely they must be around here close. You and Thomas look around while we wait here."

Miriam and Melody lost all track of time once they were in the midway. "Look at that Melody! For ten cents we can see a two-headed calf? Wonder where they found him. Let's go in and see this. Bet it's just a stuffed animal," Miriam laughed.

The tent was crowded, but Miriam and Melody managed to squeeze through to the front. "It is a live calf! Poor thing. How does he know which head to eat with?" Melody asked.

Back out on the midway, Melody suggested, "Let's get some cotton candy, Miriam. It is so much fun to eat. It sticks to your nose and everything."

They were eating the cotton candy from the paper cones. Miriam exclaimed, "Look at your dress! You have that sticky stuff all over the front, Melody. Why did you wear that beautiful dress today? You may have ruined it."

"Oh, it's not new. I was tired of it anyway. Come on, we're here to have fun."

Walking along eating the cotton candy, and laughing at all the funny carnival venders, they came to a man shouting into a megaphone, "Get your balloon rides here. Another ride going up in ten minutes. Only 25¢. Come on, girls. The chance of a lifetime! See all of Wichita from the air. You will have plenty of excitement to tell everyone back home."

"Let's go, Melody. I want to try something daring," Miriam begged, as she looked at the large fabric balloons filled with hot air, attached to a wicker basket hanging below for passengers.

"But Miriam, we are supposed to be back to go to the circus. You know your parents wouldn't approve of you doing anything like this. I'm the one who thinks of the mischief."

"Well, I'm going. Are you going to stand here and watch, or go with me?" Miriam asked.

"I'll go. You know we are to stay together. But I know

we will both be in trouble once our parents find out," Melody said.

"Come on, get out your money. They are loading now, and they can only take six people in the gondola each time," Miriam pushed.

Aaron and Thomas were rushing around the midway looking for the girls. Aaron looked into a tent, "How can they disappear so quickly?" Thomas asked. "Your Miriam is always so dependable. I knew she could be depended on to keep Melody straight. That is why I allowed Melody to sit with her during the speech."

"Yes, Miriam is always so dependable. I guess I just took her for granted. I can't imagine where they would be. There is such a crowd here that it would be impossible to see them even if they were close."

The hot air balloon was lifting off as Thomas and Aaron came running past. Melody poked Miriam, "Look! She whispered, "There are our fathers. They are looking for us. Should we call to them? They don't see us."

"Shush. I want to enjoy this view without them demanding that the operators bring the balloon right back down. We'll be back in a little while," Miriam answered stubbornly. They were soon high up over Wichita. "Look at this view. It's magnificent! Look at those little bugs running around. Oh! That must be the people. There is the circus tent over there. I feel like a bird. I'm flying."

"Miriam, I can't believe you are acting this way. You've always been so proper and sure about what I should do. What has gotten into you?"

"Sometimes I just want to be different. You know that I really didn't want to move out to western Kansas. I still

162

miss Kansas City, Melody," Miriam answered.

"Oh! Look out! The balloon is tipping," Melody screamed, "We're going down fast! I'm scared," Melody cried.

"Hang on to me, Melody. Let's pray that God will protect us. What if we crash? Why did I ever talk you into going on this trip? Now it will be my fault if we both get killed."

Melody's face was white as snow, and her eyes big as saucers. Clinging to Miriam she sobbed, "I'm so scared. How can you be so calm?"

"I'm scared too. I feel like I'm going to vomit. I wish the others would quit screaming. How can the man think what he is doing, with all that screaming?"

The balloonist worked furiously, throwing over sand bags so that the balloon would ascend, but he quickly announced, "Sorry, ladies and gentleman but we are going to have to land out here in the country. We will see that you get back to the fair, but it will be a while before our crew finds us."

Aaron had seen the girls in the balloon gondola. "Look, Thomas, there they are. Let's ask if there is some way they can bring it back now."

"I know they can't bring them back that soon. I've ridden those before. But we can ask when they will return," Thomas responded. "We should go back and tell Lydia and Mary so they won't be worried. Maybe we could send them with the little girls to the circus."

"We had better be here when the girls return, so we make sure they don't go elsewhere," Aaron advised. Mary took one look at Thomas' ashen face, "Thomas, what is wrong?

You are sweating so heavily. You must get back to the hotel to lie down. Maybe we can find a doctor to look at you."

Aaron helped Thomas back to the hotel. Once lying down, he was breathing a little easier, but the pains in his chest continued. "I think it's my heart. You better find a doctor." Aaron went to the lobby and asked the manager, "Where can we find a doctor quickly? Mr. Cramton may be having a heart attack."

"I will call Dr. Black, he has an office in the next block. He can come quickly," the manager answered.

Aaron ran back up the stairs to Thomas' room. "The doctor will be here soon," he told Mary as she bathed Thomas' head with cool cloths.

Thomas said, "Aaron, if I don't survive this, will you take care of Mary and Melody? I have set up trusts for them at the Beloit Bank."

Crying softly, Mary said, "I'm not worried about money now, Thomas. I just want to know that you will be in heaven when I get there."

Thomas said, "I know that I need Christ. I have run from Him so long. I thought I could handle any problem myself, but I am afraid of dying. Aaron would you help me pray the prayer for an old sinner like me?" Aaron led, and Thomas prayed after him. "Dear God, I know I'm a sinner. I know my sin deserves to be punished. I believe Christ died and rose from the grave for me. I trust Jesus Christ as my Savior. Thank You for giving me everlasting life, and for forgiving my sin. Amen."

"Now I feel like a load has been lifted off me. If I died right now, I know that I am right with God, and I would go right to heaven."

There was a knock on the door, and Lydia opened the door to find a man standing there, "I'm Dr. Black. You called for me?"

"Yes, we think that Mr. Cramton may be having a heart attack. Come right in."

Dr. Black listened to Thomas' chest for a few minutes and took his pulse. "I don't think you have had a heart attack, but I could be wrong. I would suggest complete bed rest for you for a few weeks. You have over stressed your heart. If you need a place to stay, we have homes here in Wichita where you and your family could stay while you recuperate."

"I need to make sure my daughter is all right before we make any plans. Aaron, get a carriage and go back to the carnival. Those girls will have no idea where we are. I will rest better knowing that you are with them," Thomas said.

As Aaron left, he heard Thomas asking the doctor, "Could I stand the train ride back to Beloit with my family? I would rest better in my own home," Thomas asked.

"Yes, if you can lie down, I think the trip home would not hurt you, but you need to completely stay away from your job for at least six weeks, or you may have a heart attack," Dr. Black announced.

"I have capable help at the newspaper. I think they can put out the paper for a few weeks. Thank you for coming, doctor."

Aaron found the balloon ride booth, and rushed to ask the announcer, "Hasn't the balloon returned? Our daughters were on it. What happened? It was to be back in thirty minutes," Aaron cried.

"Hold on, Mister. There has been some problem. We have sent a carriage out to look for the balloon. Sometimes they have to land outside of town. I'm sure everything is all right. Just sit down here and wait. I will give you word as soon as I hear."

"Oh Lord, take care of those girls. Thomas can't stand anymore trouble today. Bring them back safely," Aaron prayed.

It seemed like hours before the carriage from the city arrived to pick up the balloon riders. "Our parents are going to be frantic with worry, Miriam. And it is all your fault. Father will not let me out of the house for a year, and it's all because of you," Melody fumed.

"But wasn't it fun? You enjoyed it too. And no one was hurt," Miriam replied.

"Now you are sounding like me. What has gotten into you? You are the one who told me that we should obey our parents because God said so. Now look at the mess you got us into," Melody sobbed.

"Oh, all right. I made a wrong choice. Our parents are probably worried sick. I didn't think anything would happen. I need to ask God's forgiveness for my disobedience. You know He says if we will admit our sins, He forgives," Miriam said.

"But what about the problems we caused our parents? Will they go away just because God forgives?" Melody asked.

"No, that is right. Our parents are probably worried sick, and they may make us stay away from each other for several weeks. Maybe forever. I didn't think it would turn out like this," Miriam said soberly.

Aaron was waiting for the girls at the balloon booth. He looked so sad and worried. Miriam ran up and hugged him, "We're back safe and sound, Father. Why are you looking so sad?"

"Miriam, I'm shocked that you would disobey us and cause all this trouble. Melody's father was so upset that he almost had a heart attack worrying about you girls. He is back at the hotel. Come get into the carriage and we will join the rest of the family so we can make plans to return home," Aaron announced. He grabbed her arm strongly. "Come with me." Miriam started to cry.

Melody asked Aaron, "Mr. Jensen, is my father going to die? He isn't ready to meet God."

"Your father is resting quietly. He asked me to pray with him at the hotel. He told me that he was ready to believe that Jesus died for his sins. The doctor didn't think he has had a heart attack, but said that he needed lots of rest for the next few weeks."

"My father accepted Jesus! Did you hear that, Miriam? That is what we have been praying for. Oh, thank you for telling me, Mr. Jensen," Melody said through sobbing tears of joy.

Back at the hotel, Melody ran to her father's room. "Oh Father, Mr. Jensen told me you accepted Jesus. I'm sorry we disobeyed your orders and caused you all that trouble. Was that why you had the heart attack?"

"I have been running from God, and so angry at everything, Melody. Finding that you had disobeyed me just added to my anger. It was too hard on my heart. I have peace with God now, so my recovery will go much quicker."

Aaron asked, "Shall I call the train station and ask for a Pullman for your trip home, Thomas?"

"Yes, Aaron, do that now so we will all be able to leave as planned tomorrow. As soon as you finish, I want you to take Melody and your family and walk about the fair. I have about ruined the fun for you. I will be all right here with Mary. We can leave as planned tomorrow morning."

"If you are sure you will be all right. I know the little girls are looking forward to the circus," Aaron commented.

"I want to stay with Father," Melody announced. I am so glad that our whole family is Christian now. You don't know how hard I have prayed for that. That is the best part of our trip." Melody fell down beside her father and hugged him.

"Now, you go with Mr. and Mrs. Jensen and the girls, and see the rest of the fair. I will be all right here with Mother. The doctor says I just need rest for several weeks."

Melody ran to catch up with Miriam. "Oh, Miriam, our prayers for Father are answered! He is a child of God now. I am so happy. Now we can be a real family, like yours."

CHAPTER FOURTEEN

CHANGES

IT HAD BEEN A LONG tiring day at the fair. Aaron had taken them to the evening circus which the children enjoyed thoroughly, especially the clown and animal acts. Miriam and Melody were more concerned about the problems of the day. "I hope Father will recover from these heart problems," Melody whispered. "I've caused him so much unhappiness with my stubbornness. Now that he has accepted Christ, I don't want anything to happen to him, so we can start over."

"Melody, we both have been stubborn and caused our parents problems, but they have forgiven us and so will God. Growing up can sometimes be fun, but at other times it is frightening. We have choices all the time, every day. I know I made several bad ones today, and I probably will make many more. Father will not trust me as much as he did, because I disobeyed him today. But let's get off this serious talk. We came to enjoy the circus. I've never see a circus before."

A talented tightwire walker had just started her performance. "Ooooo, look at her!" Jesse squealed. "I wish I could do that!"

The announcer introduced the performers, "This is the Walmsley family from New York. Carilla, the youngest, is only thirteen and she has been performing with her family since she was eight years old."

Melody looked at Miriam. "That would be an exciting life, to travel all over the country and perform to cheering crowds. You would never have a dull moment."

The announcer told more about the family, "The Walmsley family spends six hours a day perfecting their act. Carilla started learning the basics of tightwire walking when she was three. She does all her schooling after practice each day. Watch her perform this very difficult act with her parents."

Everyone held their breath as Carilla stood on the shoulders of her parents who walked the long wire. "Oh, she's wonderful," Jesse exclaimed. "Could I start practicing for that Father? I'm four years old."

Aaron started to answer just as Carilla finished her difficult performance. The crowd broke into thunderous applause. As she left the tent, Carilla walked in front of Melody and Miriam. "She doesn't look very happy," Melody whispered to Miriam. "She doesn't look like she even hears the applause and the cheers."

"Melody, would you enjoy practicing day after day for a ten minute performance, and never having a home of your own?" Lydia asked, leaning down from the second row.

"It would be fun for a while. I could travel and see new places," Melody mused.

"No, you can't join the circus, Melody, I need you in Beloit. Don't go escaping without me," Miriam laughed.

The little girls were asleep in Lydia and Aaron's arms as they left the circus.

Back at the hotel, Melody found her mother still sitting by Thomas' bed. "He's resting peacefully. He told me that he is so thankful that he is right with God and didn't know why he had been running from God all these years. He seems much more peaceful than he has been in years. He told me that things will be different in our family once he is recovered," Mary joyfully reported.

"But Mother, I've caused both of you so much trouble. How can I ever undo the trouble I have caused?" Melody asked sorrowfully.

"We are going to go on from here, Honey. We all have so much to learn, but with God's help, we will make a new start in our family life. Now, get some sleep so you will be ready to leave in the morning," Mary requested.

Thomas slept most of the way home to Beloit. Mary stayed in the Pullman with him until noon. Melody asked her mother about dinner, "Do you want Aaron to help roll your wheelchair to the buffet car, Mother? We children are hungry."

"Yes, Melody. I can leave your father for a few minutes. Ask Aaron to help me out of here."

As they were eating, Mary said, "There is no way that I can keep Thomas home and resting, unless someone he trusts is running the paper. Harold is a good reporter, but he has never put out the whole paper by himself. I would have to tie Thomas in his bed to keep him home, and he still wouldn't rest for worrying about the paper."

"Could we find someone to fill in during this time?" Aaron asked.

"That would be difficult on short notice," Mary answered. "Thomas thinks that he is the only one who can put the paper out. He has worked when he was so sick that I despaired for his life, but he wouldn't listen to me."

"I just remembered that our new pastor told me that he had published a Christian newspaper before he moved here. I wonder if Rev. Stanwick would consider filling in for Thomas for six weeks," Aaron suggested.

"Can you talk to him the minute we arrive home so that Thomas won't go to the office? I know that once the train stops, he will be asking Jackson to take him by the office."

It was mid afternoon when the train pulled into the station. Melody looked out the window and saw Harold from the newspaper. "Oh, no, he must not talk to father," she exclaimed to Miriam. "Tell your father to keep my father in here until I can send Harold back to the office."

Melody ran out the door to where Harold was waiting in his carriage. "Harold, Father has almost had a heart attack. The doctor said he must have complete rest for six weeks. Whatever you are here, for don't tell Father...."

"But, there has been a bank robbery at the Beloit State Bank this morning. I need your father's help to get that story in the morning's paper. The bank president wouldn't tell me all the details. Said he wanted to talk to Mr. Cramton first."

"You must not tell Father. We will think of something. Please go before Father sees you. As soon as we get him home, Mr. Jensen and I will come down to the office. Mr. Jensen has someone in mind who might be able to help."

Harold drove off muttering to himself, "The boss won't like this. He always wants to report the exciting accounts himself. He won't like it, he won't like it...."

174

Melody ran over to where Jackson was waiting in the Cramton's carriage. "Father almost had a heart attack. We must get him home as quickly as possible, without stressing him. Mr. Jensen is helping him out of the train. Come get our luggage and Mother so we can leave immediately for home."

Jackson obeyed without a word. Regardless of his grumpy attitude, he cared a lot for the Cramton's. Jackson and Aaron soon had Thomas sitting in the back seat of the carriage. "I can carry your luggage, Mr. Jensen, but there isn't room for all your family. Do you want me to come back for you?" Jackson asked.

"No, we can walk from here. It would do us good after the long ride. Bring the luggage by after you have Mr. Cramton safely resting. Melody and I will need a ride out to Rev. Stanwick's farm, and then to the newspaper office.

At home Lydia and the girls changed to their work dresses, and Aaron to work clothes. They fed and watered the chickens and calf. Lydia said, "Anna, will you watch Emma and Tabitha so Miriam can help me pick tomatoes and cucumbers before it gets dark?"

"Yes, Mother, if you will take Jessie with you. She will insist that I read *Peter Rabbit* to her for the fiftieth time, and I am so tired of that story."

"Come with us, Jessie. You can carry the bucket for the tomatoes. That will speed up our picking," Lydia said.

Jackson and Melody came for Aaron after a few minutes. "Help me unload your luggage and we will be off to find the Reverend," Jackson said. Aaron hadn't heard Jackson talk that much before. He thought Mr. Cramton's illness must really be bothering him.

"Drive by the church first, Reverend Stanwick might be studying there," Aaron advised.

Aaron jumped down from the carriage before it stopped at the church, and was bounding up the steps just as the door opened and a surprised Reverend Stanwick was almost knocked down as Aaron came through the door. "Reverend, we need help from you immediately. Can you come with us so I can explain our problem?" Aaron asked breathlessly.

"If you can explain what you are talking about, I would be better able to tell you if I can help," Rev. Stanwick answered.

Melody turned around from the front seat and said, "We need an editor for the newspaper tonight. My father, Mr. Cramton, has almost had a heart attack. He is to have complete bed rest for six weeks. When we arrived in town this afternoon, Harold, father's reporter, said there had been a bank robbery this morning. He knew my father would want the story in tomorrow's paper. Can you help Harold get the story from the bank president and help us print the paper tonight?"

"Yes, we must keep Thomas from worrying over the paper now that he is home," Aaron added.

Reverend Stanwick sighed, "Well, I've never been asked to write about such an exciting event before. I will be glad to do what I can. Aaron, I will need your prayers that God will help me know how to do this. Let's get to the office and talk to Harold. I need more details."

Harold was in such a dither when they arrived. "What am I going to do without Mr. Cramton? No one can do this story but him. He will fire me. I know he will, for not telling him...."

"Harold, I hear that you are the good reporter here," Reverend Stanwick said. "Maybe between us we can put the paper out tonight. How do we get the details on the bank robbery?"

"Well, Mr. Johnson, the bank president, was so upset this morning that he said, 'When Thomas gets back, I will give him the story.' I don't know if he will trust anyone else."

"Grab your hat and take me over to Mr. Johnson's home. We will get our story. Melody, do you know something about running this place? Is there something you can do while we are gone?"

"Yes, Reverend Stanwick, I do typesetting for Father. I can start on the regular news while you are gone. Mr. Jensen will stay with me. Be sure to tell Mr. Johnson why my father can't come. It will take a miracle to keep Father out of this office for six weeks."

Melody worked for an hour or more before Reverend Stanwick and Harold returned. "That was quite a robbery. Mr. Johnson was most helpful once he heard about Thomas' illness. Now, let's see if I can write this story the way Thomas would have," Reverend Stanwick said.

They worked late into the night, and, by midnight, had the paper all printed for morning delivery. Thomas would be proud of them. "Reverend Stanwick, you are some newspaper man! I'd never have believed anyone could come in here and replace Mr. Cramton," Harold announced. "Mighty nice of you to help out."

"I have told Aaron that if you can put up with me, and Mr. Cramton agrees, I can fill in during this time when he is ill. It has been good to put my training back to work," Reverend Stanwick responded.

The next morning, when Thomas sent Jackson to pick up the morning paper, he was surprised. "Who wrote this? When did it happen? Listen to this, Mary. The local bank was broken into sometime between 1 a.m. and 4 a.m. The safe and vault were blown open with dynamite and nitroglycerine. Two thousand, four hundred seventy dollars, in currency, silver, gold, and postage stamps were taken. The safe had been in use for seven years, and was supposed to be burglar proof."

Mary smiled, "Didn't Reverend Stanwick, Melody, Harold, and the staff do a good job? See, you don't have to worry about the paper these six weeks. You can stay here and rest."

"But I don't know anything about the Reverend Stanwick," Thomas grumbled. "Who is he anyway? Just because he put out one good paper doesn't mean he can keep doing it everyday."

"Would you like to meet him? I've invited him to come for morning coffee at ten. I knew you wouldn't rest until you met him yourself. Melody and Aaron were impressed with his ability to help in the emergency."

Reverend Stanwick came as planned at ten. Jackson let him in and said, "Reverend Stanwick, good to see you again. You're a mighty great guy."

"Seems like everyone in this family knows you but me," Thomas called from the bedroom. "Would you come in? I am Thomas Cramton, the editor of the newspaper you published last night."

Reverend Stanwick smiled and gave Thomas a hearty handshake, "I understand that you might be a little worried about my abilities. My name is Robert Stanwick;

please call me Robert. When Aaron told me yesterday afternoon that they had an emergency in which he felt I could help, I told him that I would need his prayer for God's wisdom to do it correctly. If you think that I can do the job, I will try to do my best for you while you recover from your attack."

"You mean you would be willing to put out the paper for six weeks? I was absolutely sure there was no one to be found on short notice," Thomas said in surprise.

Mary smiled, "But you didn't know we were praying for someone. Aaron knew that Reverend... I mean Robert had published a Christian paper before he came here. What we didn't know yesterday, was whether he would be able to do last night's paper on short notice. That prayer was answered also."

"I don't know much about prayer, Reverend, I just became a child of God this week. I've got a lot of learning to do in that area. Maybe you could teach me some on that," Thomas smiled.

"I may need to confer with you occasionally on the newspaper, but you have a wonderful staff at the office, Thomas. It would be a pleasure to work with them. If you have spiritual questions I will try to answer them. We can help each other. I had better return to the office. They may need my assistance. Let me know if you have any suggestions. Thank you for the coffee, Mrs. Cramton."

"Just call me Mary," Mary said. "We will probably be seeing you often."

After Reverend Stanwick left, Thomas said, "I can't believe it. Who would have guessed that a preacher would be publishing my paper? What will the guys downtown think?"

"Once they know why, they will be thankful that someone could take over your job. They depend on your paper for their advertising and news. Have you thought what you should pay Reverend Stanwick for doing your job? I hear that they are only paying him $560 a year, and the Stanwicks have several children," Mary said quietly.

"Of course I plan to pay him, but I'm not sure how to go about it. Would he take payment like the rest of the staff, or is there something they need that I could provide?"

"Why don't you talk to Aaron? He probably knows more about the family. Could we have the Jensen family over for supper tomorrow night? They have been so helpful to Melody and me while you were resting on the way home, and since arriving home. I want to thank them."

"Yes, I need to talk to Aaron about so many things. It seems like I am a child when it comes to the Bible and things like that. Yes, send Jackson over with a note to invite them. It's time we did some entertaining around here. We have this big house, and have never had people in except for Melody's parties."

Melody couldn't wait for the Jensens to arrive the next evening. "Mother, can't I go to Miriam's and visit this afternoon? I haven't talked to her for two days."

Mary answered, "No, you will have plenty of time to talk this evening. Anabel could use your help in setting the table. Would you tell Jackson that we want his prettiest bouquet of roses for the table? Did Anabel find those linen napkins that match the crocheted table cloth? I can't remember where we put them."

Lydia had to hurry the little girls through their baths so she could curl their hair. "I don't know why I am so nervous over a meal with the Cramtons. We used to be invited to beautiful homes in Kansas City before we moved here. But we always left you girls at home with Auntie. Maybe that is what bothers me. I'm afraid you will spill something or make a fuss."

"No, we won't Mother. We'll be very very good," Jessie said. "I will shake Mr. Cramton's hand and then be very quiet."

"You can't keep from talking, Jessie, and you know it," Anna said. "Maybe after we eat, we children can go out to the flower garden while you adults visit. That way we won't cause as many problems for you, Mother."

"Whatever Mrs. Cramton tells you, I want you to obey. If she wants you all to sit in the parlor all evening, you are not to argue."

"This doesn't sound like a very 'joyable evening to me," Jessie pouted. "Just sittin' and listenin' to adults talk is tiresome."

"Don't start pouting, Jesse," Miriam said. "It might not be as bad as you think. Besides we had a good time with the Cramtons at the fair. Don't you remember the circus that Mr. Cramton treated us to?"

Aaron hurried home from work, bathed, and changed into his new suit. "I feel uncomfortable eating in a suit but I suppose Thomas will be wearing a suit."

At last they were ready. Jackson had told them he would arrive at six sharp to pick them up in the carriage. He arrived right on time. "Look, Jackson is smiling," Anna said. "I have never seen him smiling before."

"Maybe he is getting used to us by now," Miriam said. "Five girls are a bit difficult for a guy like him."

Thomas met them at the door as they arrived, "I told Mary that I could answer the door. I'm not that sick. Do come in, supper is ready, and I have so much to talk to you about, Aaron."

They sat at the beautiful table with white china and real silverware. Lydia kept Tabitha in her lap. "I had better feed her and then put her down. It wouldn't be safe allowing her to sit in one of your beautiful dining chairs."

"Aaron, will you say grace? I don't know much about praying yet, but I am going to learn," Thomas said.

The food was delicious, and Jessie didn't talk much at all. Lydia was pleased that the girls remembered their manners. Following a dessert of chocolate mousse, Mary said, "You girls may go out to the garden to play and talk. If you want to take Tabitha, it would be safe out there, because Jackson has all the buffalo burrs weeded out."

"Oh, thank you, Mrs. Cramton. I was afraid we would have to sit in the parlor all evening and listen to you dull adults," Jessie blurted out. Lydia looked horrified.

Mary laughed, "I know what it is like to be a little girl, and it does get tiring to listen to adult talk. You go outside and enjoy the garden. There is a croquet set out there for you to play together. Melody can teach you how to play it. She never has anyone to play with her, except Jackson, so she will enjoy that."

"I want to get right to some business, Aaron," Thomas stated. "How can I best pay Reverend Stanwick for his work at the paper? Mary tells me that he only receives $560 a year."

Aaron thought a minute, "I'm not sure, but I do know that they have four children and Mrs. Stanwick is expecting another one this winter. Their house is small. Maybe building a room onto their house would be one way to help him."

"Great idea. I will call the workmen tomorrow," Thomas announced.

"Shouldn't you ask Reverend Stanwick if he wants another room first?" Mary asked. "He ought to be asked, before you send workmen out to his farm."

"You're right, of course. I keep forgetting that I'm not in charge of everyone's life," Thomas said. "I have another question, Aaron. Could you bring your violin over some evening and play some hymns for a neighborhood sing-time?"

"How did you know that I played hymns?" Aaron asked. "And who will be coming to this sing-time? I'm not very good on the violin."

"Nonsense, my daughter told me that you can play anything, and she especially loved the hymns that you played. As to who would be coming, we would put a note in the paper that anyone and everyone can come. We have a big house here. Mary can play the piano with you, if you would like. She hasn't played since we moved here, but she used to be a concert pianist before I married her. Life has changed so much for her since the accident with the horse."

"Mary, you never told me that you played the piano. Have you thought of giving lessons?" Lydia asked. "I have wanted the girls to learn the piano, but we don't have a piano, and I didn't know of anyone besides the school teacher who could teach them."

"Why, yes, I think I could give lessons. The girls

could practice here in the afternoons. I would enjoy teaching them. I never thought about it. I could give Melody lessons also. Why should I let my training at the Chicago Finishing School go to waste?" Mary said warmly. Her face almost glowed with the thought of being useful.

"Another thing, Aaron, after the sing-time I want you to teach a Bible study," Thomas said. "There are people in this town just like me. They think they are good enough to go to heaven, but they are just stubborn sinners and need God like I did. I want them to know it."

"But I am not a preacher. I have never taught a Sunday school class or led a Bible study. The only teaching I do is with my own family," Aaron protested. "Why don't you ask Reverend Stanwick? He knows how to teach."

"No, that would scare people off. They know you are a guy just like them and they like your honest way of working. They will listen to you," Thomas insisted.

"Well, I will pray about it. The singing I probably could do, but teaching a whole room full of neighbors is something else. I will talk to Reverend Stanwick about what to teach if you insist that I do it," Aaron said.

It was late when the Jensens were taken home by Jackson. "It was such an enjoyable evening," said Lydia. "The change that has come in that family since Thomas accepted Christ is truly a miracle."

"Yes, it is. The next thing we know, Thomas will be asking to be baptized in the Solomon River. He never does anything halfway. I'm sure people downtown are going to be talking about Mr. Cramton getting religion!"

Aaron was right. Thomas had Reverend Stanwick

over the next day and told him, "I want to be baptized in the river before it gets too cold. I've run from the Lord so long that it is time I get things straightened out. And I want you to start writing a Bible lesson in the paper every-day. We print all those fiction stories, but none of the truth from God's Word."

The word went around town that Thomas had gone crazy. He was staying home and letting a preacher run his paper, and had started inviting neighbors, all types and kinds, for a sing-time and Bible study.

Melody and Miriam were visiting one afternoon. Melody said, "I'm so thankful that God sent you to our town, because you and Anna came to see me even when you didn't think you were welcome. Our whole family has come to know Christ because you came, and now Mother and Father have a better marriage. There are so many mir-acles. God is a wonderful God."

"You are so right, Melody. He worked miracles for me also. I didn't like this town when we first came. We left a nice house and friends in Kansas City. God changed my attitude and gave me a wonderful friend like you."

"Do you suppose God has more surprises for us?" Melody questioned. "Since I met you, every day has been exciting. The parties that Mother used to plan for me don't even compare with my life now."

"Life may not always be this exciting just because we are Christians, but we can trust God to be in control. Father says there are no surprises with God. Wouldn't it be fun to have God tell us what is going to happen next year, or who we will marry, or where we will live."

"Didn't you tell me that your mother is going to have

a baby? Wouldn't you like to know if it will be a brother or sister?" Melody asked.

"I don't want to know that ahead of time. Either one will be fine with me. I want to know answers to the big questions. Do you realize that in five or six years we could both be married? My mother married at eighteen. We have so much to learn before then. Who do you suppose God has picked out for us?"

"You mean God has a certain boy picked out?" Melody asked in surprise. "Do you suppose William might be the one? I do miss seeing him. Why couldn't we walk down to the Ice Cream Palace to see if he and Isaac are there? I need to escape from these studies for awhile."

"Wait a minute, Melody. I haven't finished with my sermon for you. God has known everything about us since before He created the world, so why wouldn't He know? When I asked Father once about why God didn't tell us ahead of time, he told me that God wants us to take one day at a time. It would be more than we could stand if God told us everything that will happen to us even next week. Come on, we need to get back to our studies. Our mothers gave us permission to do our mathematics together, not answer all the big questions for the next five years."

"I'm tired of studies. Can't we go to the Ice Cream Palace? I'm dying for some good ice cream, and the weather is warm enough for us to walk today," Melody begged.

"You know that going to the Ice Cream Palace got us into trouble before. Remember my father reading to us at Bible study last week about fleeing from temptation."

"Pooh! You are taking all the fun out of life. If it

makes you feel better, I will ask Mother, and we can walk over to your house to ask your mother."

"But will you tell them we might see Isaac and William there? Remember, we both have our parents not trusting us. Why don't you have Jackson drive down and bring us back some ice cream, if you must have ice cream."

"No, it's not the ice cream. I want to see William. Are you going with me or not? If it will make you feel better, I will tell Mother that William and Isaac may be there," Melody unwillingly offered.

They found Mary working on lessons for her new piano students. "Mother, would you mind if Miriam and I walked down to the Ice Cream Palace? Miriam said that I must tell you that William and Isaac will probably be there. Now, I've told you, so may we go?"

"Yes, you may go, and take your father for a walk. He is talking of going to work half-days, so the doctor wants him to walk," Mary answered sweetly.

"Oh, Mother! Do we have to have Father with us?" Melody moaned.

"Yes, my dear. Your father and I have decided that we have given you too much freedom, which has led to temptations you can't resist. So, take your father for a walk. He will enjoy an outing with two attractive young ladies."

CHAPTER FIFTEEN

MELODY'S "NEW" FAMILY

THOMAS HAD OVERHEARD the conversation between Mary and the girls. He called out, "Get on your best dresses, girls. I'm going to show you how a real gentleman courts his lady."

"Oh no! What is Father up to now?" Melody whispered. "I've never heard him talk like this."

Miriam giggled, "Let's dress up and see what he has in mind. This might be fun."

"You're right, Miriam," Mary laughed. "Thomas has been full of original ideas lately. You girls might be in for a surprise."

"Oh, all right, Mother. Come on, Miriam. I know just the dress for you. It is blue and has a high lace collar. See, I did remember that you don't like low-necked dresses. And I have hair ribbons to match, or would you rather wear a hat?" Melody questioned.

"Show them to me and we can decide. This could be our most exciting trip downtown."

The girls hurriedly pulled out dresses, with hats to match, and capes for the chilly day. "I love this blue velvet, Melody. The hat is gorgeous. I've never worn a hat like this before. Show me how to wear it," Miriam requested.

There was a knock on the door. "Hurry girls. We must go before the weather cools. You've had thirty minutes; surely you are dressed by now."

"Coming, Father, let us grab our capes, and we will be there," Melody called.

Miriam opened the door to find Mr. Cramton dressed in his best suit and top hat. "You girls look right pert (fresh and happy). Here, let me help you with your cape," he suggested. Miriam had never had a man help her with her coat before. "Oh, thank you, Mr. Cramton. I forgot that a gentleman helps a lady with her coat. You're next, Melody."

Melody couldn't keep from giggling. "Father, you've never done all this for me before. Why are you doing it today?"

"You just wait and see. I have some surprises up my sleeve."

Telling Mary goodbye, they stepped out the door. "Why is Jackson waiting with the carriage, Father? I thought we were going to walk to give you some exercise."

"We'll do some walking, but right now I am helping you ladies into my carriage," Mr. Cramton answered. "Up with you, Miriam. You next, Melody. To the park, Jackson."

"Yes, sir. To the park we will go." Jackson smiled as if he knew Thomas had a surprise planned.

At the park near the center of town, Thomas called

out to Jackson, "Stop here, Jackson. I have some girls who wish to take a walk. Don't wait for us, we will walk home."

The park was empty and rather uninviting. Miriam said, "I love to see the trees bare of leaves in the winter. Some of these old oaks are so majestic. You can't see that in the summer. I'm glad you thought of starting our walk here, Mr. Cramton."

"It looks sad to me with the flowers and grass all dead until spring," Melody complained. "Not anything like our picnic spot for the fourth of July. The only bright spot is that perky red cardinal over there."

"Ladies, may I escort you on our walk; each take an arm and we shall start. We are going to walk about town and shop at some stores before we visit the Ice Cream Palace. Are you ready to go?"

"Yes, Father, but we didn't wear shoes for long walks. Why are we walking so far with the Ice Cream Palace in the next block?" Melody questioned.

"We have a few stops to make on the way. Stay with me and I will show you how a gentleman courts a lady," Thomas reminded her formally.

"First we are going to the flower shop. I am buying a flower for each of my ladies. Do you like roses, Miriam? I know that Melody does."

"I love roses, Mr. Cramton, but you don't have to buy me one. I know that they are expensive," Miriam said.

"Remember, I am showing you how a gentleman courts a lady. Right in here, ladies. Tell the clerk which color of rose you wish to wear with your dress," Thomas requested.

"These are beautiful, Mr. Cramton. Oh, thank you so

much," Miriam said gratefully. Melody looked annoyed.

"Our next stop is at the perfume counter of New York Mercantile. What is your favorite perfume, Miriam?" Thomas asked.

"You've already spent too much on me, Mr. Cramton. I've never even worn perfume. You don't have to buy any for me," Miriam said.

"You would like Gardinia, Miriam. That is what I usually purchase. Get her a bottle of that, Father. I know she will like it." Melody suggested.

"Would you like to try some of our samples, ladies? We have several new ones from Paris. Hold out your wrist, and I will put a dash on for you to smell," the overdressed clerk gushed.

"No, I think we will take the Gardinia, Madam. They don't need to smell like a perfume factory," Thomas said. "Wrap it up and we will be on our way."

"Let's walk a few more blocks and come back to the Ice Cream Palace. By that time your friends should be there. School was out about thirty minutes ago," Thomas announced.

"Father, why do you want to arrive when our friends will?" Melody asked.

"I have my reasons. You will find out soon enough."

"You aren't going to embarrass me, are you, Father? You know that Isaac and William already think I am angry with them, since I haven't spoken to them since we came back from Kansas City," Melody reminded him.

"Let me take care of it. I think you will enjoy our time," Thomas said. "Remember, I want to show you how a gentleman courts a lady."

They arrived at the Ice Cream Palace a few minutes after Isaac and William arrived. Miriam watched them intently as Mr. Cramton guided the girls to their table. Isaac's eyes grew as big as saucers but he didn't say a word. "Gentlemen, may these young ladies and I join you at your table?" Mr. Cramton asked."

"You mean us? Yea, yes, you- you m-m-may Mr. Cramton," Isaac stammered, his face turning beet red.

Mr. Cramton took Miriam's cape to hang it up, and seated her opposite the boys. "Now, Melody, let me seat you before I hang up your cape." Returning to seat himself at the head of the table, Mr. Cramton eyed the boys who squirmed nervously. "Gentlemen, I understand that you wish to court these young ladies." Melody looked at her father in shock.

"Court? That's the word Miriam used on our trip to Kansas City," Isaac said sheepishly. "No, Mr. Cramton, I don't know about William, but I'm not wanting to court nobody. We went to Kansas City with the girls because you paid for the tickets. It would be ridiculous for us to think of courting. We still have several years of school left."

"Why do you ask that, Mr. Cramton?" William asked nervously.

"I wanted the girls and you to know how a gentleman courts the woman whom he is intending to marry."

"But we aren't wanting to get married, Mr. Cramton," Isaac responded stubbornly. "Why do you think that we are?"

Acting as if he hadn't heard Isaac, Mr. Cramton continued. "First, a young man asks the girl's father for permission to come courting, and if the father, and sometimes

194

the mother, approve of the young man, he may come at certain times and join the family at meals, or to visit in the parlor."

"Mr. Cramton, we are not planning on courting these girls," William said strongly.

"You aren't? But you have encouraged them to join you here at the Ice Cream Palace, and you both took Melody out for a walk during the barn dance. I would call that showing more than the usual friendship. You've never asked my permission to spend time with my daughter, and you have taken her away from her home and my protection. This is serious business boys. From now on, if you wish to see my daughter, or Miriam, you must talk to me, or Miriam's father," Mr. Cramton said looking intently at the boys. "Do you understand?"

"You can be sure I won't be courting Melody, Mr. Cramton. If I have to go through all that to get married, I ain't goin' a marry nobody. Let's go Isaac," William answered nervously, scraping his chair back to leave.

"Sit down, William. I have a story to tell you that I recently read in the Bible. You see I am a new Christian, so I am learning these stories for the first time. You boys probably already know the story of Isaac," Mr. Cramton said.

"You mean to tell me there is someone in the church book with my name?" Isaac asked.

"There sure is, Isaac, but he was older than you in the story I am going to relate, and he wasn't a scalawag (worthless) person like some of the people in Canaan," Mr. Cramton said.

"Isaac was forty years old, and it was time for him to marry, but Abraham, his very old father, didn't want him to marry the girls in the land, because they didn't worship the true God. Abraham sent a trusted servant to the land where his relatives lived, to find a wife for Isaac. Isaac wasn't asked to go along. The old servant asked God to show him the right one, and that he would know by her willingness to give him and all his camels water. The beautiful girl who came to the well when he arrived days later, was named Rebecca, and she did offer him water, and poured water for all his camels. That was a lot of water! The old servant stopped right there and thanked God for showing him the right girl. He asked her family if she could be Isaac's wife and if they could leave the next day. They agreed, and she agreed, so they sent her with her maidservant. After many days of riding the camel, they saw Isaac in a field. He came right to Rebecca and married her right then and there. He knew that God had picked her out. How do you like that true story of courtship, Isaac and William?"

"Man alive! That was some story! I didn't know there was stories in the church book like that," William said in surprise.

"Do you boys go to church anywhere? It would be a good idea for you to get into a church so you can learn about God. Don't wait until you get old like me to follow God's lessons from the Bible," Thomas said earnestly.

"I've only been to church once, Mr. Cramton. That was at Christmas last year when my grannie took me. My old man doesn't like church. Says there is too many hypo something there," Isaac answered.

Mr. Cramton laughed, "The word is hypocrites, Isaac. Well, your father is right. There are a lot of people who don't live like Christians in church, but Jesus came to die for the sins of all of us hypocrites. Could I have Jackson pick you gentlemen up next Sunday for Sunday school? We drive near your homes about nine o'clock."

"I'd have to ask Pop. Mom has been telling him she wants to go to church but he tells her he doesn't want to hear nothin' about that religion stuff," William answered.

"You ask your parents and let me know. Right now I am treating everyone to ice cream. What flavor do you like?" Mr. Cramton asked.

After the boys had eaten and left, and the girls were alone with Thomas, Melody asked. "Why did you do that, Father? You didn't really think that William would want to court me, did you?" Melody asked.

"I knew they weren't interested in courting or marriage, but I wanted them to realize that if they do wish to see you, they will have to have my permission, and they will come to our house to visit you. I have finally realized that God has made me your protector until I give you to the young man God has for you to marry. I have neglected my responsibility too long, and I am sorry. I plan to make that up to you. May I walk you ladies home?" Mr. Cramton said cheerfully.

Later, while changing their clothes in Melody's room, Miriam said, "That was wonderful of your father. My father has told me some about courting but I didn't know that the Bible had stories about courting for our example."

"But William will never come ask Father to visit me. I'll probably never see him again. I know Father won't allow us to go to the Ice Cream Palace alone again," Melody complained.

"Melody, you should be thankful that your father is

197

wanting to be your protector. Our fathers know a lot more than we do about who would be a good husband. Don't you trust your father to choose someone who would be a Christian and good for you?" Miriam asked.

"Well, your father has been studying the Bible a lot longer than my father. And you are used to doing things that way. I'm not sure I trust my father to choose the right husband for me. He will probably find some newspaper editor like himself. I like making my own choices," Melody pouted.

Just before Thanksgiving, Thomas came home from a half-day at work to announce, "I'm ready to work full-time now, but I am going to keep Reverend Stanwick on part-time. He has become a wonderful friend and counselor. I have asked him to work as much as he has time, and to write a daily Bible lesson for the Gazette. We've printed those fiction stories for years; now it is time to print some quality material.

"Did the workmen finish the addition to the Stanwick's house?" Mary asked.

"Yes, they finished a week or two before the baby arrived. Mrs. Stanwick sent word by Robert that she is so thankful for the extra room. I'm glad that you thought of it."

Mary invited the Jensens for Thanksgiving dinner. The invitation from Mary Cramton read: "I want to thank God for your family and the wonderful help you have been to us this year. Our life has changed so much. If you could bring two of your delicious pumpkin pies, we can add that to Thomas' favorite of Boston baked beans like his mother bakes."

Snow had begun to fall the day before Thanksgiving. Miriam didn't enjoy going out for wood for the stove and vegetables from the cellar. "I hate going into that root cellar, Mother. There is a rat in there. He scares me to death. Couldn't Father bring these things in for you before he goes to work?"

"If the baby wasn't due in February, I would do it myself, Honey. The fresh air will do you good. You said you were tired of being inside all day. Take the broom to scare the rat outside. Put the tom cat inside before you leave; that might encourage mister rat to feed on something besides our vegetable supply. Besides, you need the practice, as you will be doing more of the cooking and washing as it gets closer to the time for the baby."

Miriam shoveled the snow away from the door, and carried the kerosene lantern into the moldy-smelling cellar. It was so spooky with all the shadows. "Ugg, it smells like something dead in here." Miriam ran out the door screaming. Running into the house, she slammed the door behind her and stood there panting. "I'm never going in that place again. I think there is a dead body down there; the smell is horrible."

"Miriam, did you look to see what was dead? We can't leave it in there. It probably is that rat. Now march right back there and find out. Take the shovel and carry it out behind the barn. That is our food supply for the winter, so we can't have something dead in there."

"But Mother, the smell is terrible. What if it is one of our cats. I couldn't stand to find one of them. Please let Father do it when he comes home."

"No, Miriam, I need those pumpkins now, and it will

be dark when your Father arrives home. You will have a lot more difficult jobs in the years ahead."

By the time her father arrived home, Miriam had taken the dead rat out back, and her mother had the pumpkins on cooking for the pies.

Jackson arrived shortly before noon the next day to drive the Jensen family to the Cramton home. "Mr. Cramton said there was no use of you getting out your cutter. (Large highsided sled pulled by horses) May I help you ladies into the cutter? Wrap these buffalo robes across you to keep out the cold. There's hot bricks on the floor to keep your feet warm and toasty. All ready for that Thanksgiving feast?"

Mary truly had a feast prepared. There was turkey stuffed with chestnut stuffing, giblet gravy, cranberry sauce, and mincemeat pie, along with the pumpkin pies that Lydia had baked.

After the meal, Thomas shocked everyone with an announcement, "I want to invite the whole town here for Christmas."

"But, Thomas, we can't hold all the town in here, besides the churches have celebrations and programs," Mary protested.

"I want the whole world to know that God has turned me around, and that it is Christ's birthday we are celebrating."

"Why don't you put a full-page ad in the Gazette, Father? You could tell about how God turned you around," Melody suggested.

"Yes, I could do that, but I want to do more. Can't we think of something we could do to show our love for God and His people?" Thomas asked.

Aaron looked puzzled, "I don't know exactly what you have in mind, Thomas. Let me think about it awhile, and our family will be praying about what to do."

Right after Thanksgiving, a blizzard hit. It snowed for two days; blowing snow drifted several feet high. Even the trains couldn't get through for a few days. After the snow stopped, the wind continued to blow, howling around the corners of the house so that the only warm place was right near the stove in the kitchen. Miriam sat by the window grumbling, "I can't even visit with Melody. I'm so tired of being stuck inside this house."

"You could go out to the barn and check on the cows and horses, if you want something to do, Miriam. They probably need extra hay and grain with this cold. Your father said that he would be home early since he didn't have much work, and he didn't want to wait until dark to come home. Old Ginger knows the way, but it would be easy to get lost with everything covered with snow and the wind still blowing."

Miriam bundled up tightly, "Anything beats sitting in here all day. Maybe I can find a cat to talk to out there."

"Come right back so I won't worry about you. I will need your help with supper," Lydia called as Miriam went out the door.

Anna and Jessie were playing checkers when the door suddenly burst open. "Papa, why are you home so early?" Anna asked.

"Because it is so cold and the snow so deep, I was concerned about you here not having enough wood. Where is Miriam, she can help me bring in more wood."

"She went to check on the cows and horses in the

barn about thirty minutes ago. Mama told her to come right back, but she hasn't. She's probably out there talking to my kitten," Jessie whimpered.

"I wonder why she hasn't come back by now. Tell Mother that I'm going out to the barn to find Miriam," Aaron said as he hurried out the door.

Miriam had gone to the barn and seeing that the cows had water and enough feed she thought, "It doesn't seem real cold and the wind has gone down. I could walk to Melody's and be back before anyone missed me."

Once out on the road, the wind was much stronger, but Miriam kept walking. There was a track through the drifts where some sleighs had gone through. "I can walk a mile in this. It isn't that bad."

Aaron trudged through the snow to the barn and called, "Miriam, Miriam, I need you to help me bring in wood. Where are you? This is no time to be hiding." There was no answer. "She's not here. There's her footprints in the snow going down the lane. She must have decided to visit Melody. She doesn't realize how fast frostbite can happen. Help me find her quickly, Oh Lord," Aaron prayed.

Miriam pushed on, determined to reach Melody's house. "I should have asked Mother for permission. I'm getting so cold, and I can't see where I'm going." Without warning, she stumbled over something in the snow, and fell into a deep drift. "Oh no! Help me, Jesus. I think I sprained my ankle, I can't walk on it. I could freeze to death, and no one would know where I was. Why, oh why, did I come out in this?" Miriam cried in pain.

Aaron followed Miriam's tracks and kept calling her name, but the wind carried his words away. Following her tracks as well as he could in the snow, he almost fell over her in his rush to find her. Miriam was crying so hard that she didn't hear him coming. "Oh Father, you found me. I was afraid I would freeze to death before anyone found me. I knew no one would know where to look for me. I'm so sorry."

"Hush now. Let's get you back home. See if you can stand, and I will support you as we try to make it back. If I hadn't followed you when I did, the wind would have covered your tracks and it would have been too dark to find you."

Holding tightly to her father, Miriam hobbled along beside him. "You may have some frostbite or chilblain (inflammation from freezing) from this, Miriam. Why did you try to go any place in this cold? I hate to think of what would have happened if I hadn't found you when I did."

Arriving home after what seemed like hours, Miriam was met at the door by an anxious Lydia, and Anna and Jessie who were crying. "Did you freeze to death? You're all covered with snow," Jessie said, "Mama had us prayin' for you."

"Help me get her boots off, and bring some wet cloths to rub her feet. They may be frozen," Aaron instructed.

"Oh, my ankle hurts so terribly! I can't stand for you to touch it!" Miriam cried.

"We have to get the boot off, Miriam, before we can see how bad it is hurt, and to stop the danger of chilblain," Aaron said. "There is no way we can stop it from hurting until we pull your boot off."

Anna helped Miriam out of her coat, and wrapped her in a blanket, while Lydia brought cold wet cloths, until circulation came back into her feet.

It was a sad evening for the family. Miriam rested with her foot up on a chair. She kept saying over and over, "I'm so sorry, I'm so sorry. I didn't think about what would happen."

"Often we have to learn the hard way, Miriam," Aaron said. "You aren't going to be able to walk on that foot for a few days. You not only sprained it, but your toes have some chilblain. I think that you may find staying in the house is the best place during the winter."

The sun came out the next day, and people were beginning to dig out. Miriam was reading by the window, and almost asleep in her chair, when, suddenly, she was jolted awake by unannounced visitors in the yard. "Oh! It's Melody. Anna, come open the door for her," Miriam called. Jackson pulled the sleigh close to the front door and Melody jumped down, carefully holding her long skirt up out of the snow.

Anna opened the door and announced, "Miriam is a cripple. You can come hold her hand."

"She's what? How did this happen, Miriam? Did you fall? Did something fall on you? I came over to ask you to my party next week and I find you like this? How did you do it, and will you be able to walk next week? I told Mother that I was going to have a conniption fit (fit of hysteria) if I didn't have someone to visit soon. That convinced her to let me plan a party for next week," Melody rushed on breathlessly.

"If you will stop asking questions, I will tell you what happened," Miriam replied. "I was so tired of being stuck in the house yesterday, that after I checked on the livestock, I decided to walk to your house," Miriam reported.

"You what? Father said it wasn't fit for man or beast to

be out yesterday. You have more sense than to do something so ridiculous. You could have frozen to death. I'm the one who is supposed to be scatter-brained," Melody responded in shock.

"I know how foolish and wrong it was. God answered my prayer for help, and Father was able to find me in time. He said I should be able to walk by next week, but someone has to keep rubbing my ankle and moving it so it won't get stiff. Both feet hurt from the chilblains, and my ankle hurts so badly that I can't put any weight on it now. Father made me a crutch so that I can move around some, but I'm no help to Mother when she needs it."

Melody stayed most of the afternoon, and Anna served as their maid, bringing them some milk and cookies. "You are an efficient maid, Anna. I almost forgot, you are invited to the party, also. It will be a Christmas party and we have invited several girls from church. I hope the weather will improve by then."

Miriam felt encouraged after Melody left. "Now, if I can just get these chilblains and my ankle healed up."

Aaron arrived home from work with some good news. "I talked with Dr. Kellogg when he came for some work on his sleigh this afternoon. He said that chilblains can be cured by putting the feet first in a bucket of hot water, and then in very cold water four or five times. He said to repeat the treatment every night before retiring for bed."

The weather did clear up some the week of the party. Miriam was able to walk, but not without pain. "I'm afraid this will be a sit-down party for me. I know she hasn't invited boys, so I won't be expected to dance. Anna, can you iron that blue velvet that Melody gave me? My ankle hurts too much for me to press it, and Mother shouldn't do it."

Miriam had to wear extra pairs of stockings inside her woolen ones, to protect her feet since they were extremely sensitive to cold. "Will my feet ever get so they don't hurt so much in the cold, Father?" Miriam asked.

"I did almost the same thing when I was your age, and it was several years before I could stand to be out in the cold very long without terrible pain. I guess it was a reminder that disobedience has a cost. I'm thankful neither of us lost any toes," Aaron answered.

Jackson came for the girls at seven. Anna was so excited to be going to her first party. "Help me with this hair bow, Miriam. I can't get it straight. Does my dress look all right? I'm so nervous."

"You both look very nice, girls," Lydia said. "Now have a good time, and help Mrs. Cramton if she needs it. She was so nice to allow Melody to have this party, with Thomas planning one for the whole town."

Aaron stopped her and said, "I don't think he will have a party for the whole town. He has decided to deliver food to the poor families, and has asked me to help him. We both felt there were already too many parties in town, but not many of the poor families receive gifts."

Driving up the lane to the Cramton's, Anna exclaimed. "Oh! Look at that tree in the window. It must have a thousand candles. It's beeeeeautiful! I've never seen a tree like that!"

Inside, Melody, her mother, and Anabel, the maid, had decorated the whole house with greenery, and glass balls of every color. Miriam stood and stared. "You have made this so Christmasy. Where did you find the carved stable with Mary, Joseph and baby Jesus? They are almost life-like."

"Thomas found that in Kansas City last week where he did our Christmas shopping, and met with some editors about some plans he is making for the paper," Mary answered.

Melody invited the girls to gather around the piano and sing Christmas songs while she played. Mary, who was sitting behind them said, "You sound so melodious, Miriam, has anyone told you that you are blessed with a very excellent singing voice? Have you thought of taking singing lessons? I could help you some on that."

"Do you mean that, Mrs. Cramton? I've concentrated on learning the violin so much that I hadn't thought about voice lessons. We sing as a family some, but just for fun."

"I'll talk to your mother about this after the baby arrives and life settles down a little for your family," Mary smiled.

Melody had games and a Christmas Bible lesson for the girls, and small gifts for each one. Anabel served a delicious cherry dessert. "I wish we could have parties like this more often," Anna said.

"Could we, Mother?" Melody asked, "This is so much more fun than those parties you used to plan for me. Could we have some kind of party each month and invite other girls? In the summer we could meet out in the garden."

"Why, yes. I think that might be something we could do. Let me talk to your father and Miriam's mother and the other mothers."

The moon shown brightly on the snow as the girls

were taken home by Jackson. "Take us home last, Jackson," Anna begged. "It is so pretty out here."

Winter storms came through again, and Miriam was stuck at home but she was learning to be content. Near the first of February, she was doing most of the housework. Lydia was in bed resting much of the time, for the baby was due to arrive soon. One afternoon, they were alone while the other girls napped. Lydia said, "Miriam, I have asked Mrs. Polinsky to come when it is time for the baby to arrive. She is to come next week to bring some supplies to have on hand, and to check to see how soon the baby will arrive. She knows more than any doctor, according to the women I've talked to in town. I want you to come listen to her, and learn what she does, because a winter storm could keep her from arriving in time."

Mrs. Polinsky arrived one morning between storms. She was short and heavy set. She came shuffling in out of the cold. "Sure don't like this cold none. Makes my arthritis flare up. Where's your mama, young lady? Gotta see when that baby is gonna arrive." Miriam led her into the bedroom.

"Mother is in here, Mrs. Polinsky," Miriam said.

After Mrs. Polinsky checked Lydia, she announced. "That baby is going to arrive mighty soon, could even be tonight, and there's a storm a comin'. I can feel it in my bones. Do you think Aaron can deliver the baby if I can't get here?"

"He probably would go for Dr. Kellogg, because I don't think he wants to deliver a baby. I don't want Dr. Kellogg. This is woman's work. That is why I told Miriam that I want you to tell her what to do in case you are not here in time. What does she need to have ready?"

Mrs. Polinsky looked down her chubby nose and said, "You're not very old to be delivering babies, but here are some things you need to have on hand, and be sure to keep hot water heating on the stove 'cause you need plenty of that."

"Couldn't you just stay here tonight, Mrs. Polinsky? I know Father would want you to if you could," Miriam asked.

"No, my old man wouldn't hear to that. He wants his supper, and the cow milked. We're only a mile out of town so your Father won't have far to come if that storm doesn't arrive," Mrs. Polinsky said, as she shuffled to the door.

After Mrs. Polinsky left, Miriam stirred supper and prayed as she had never prayed before, "Dear Lord, please hold back the storm so that Mrs. Polinsky can be here to deliver the baby. I know how to help, and Mother doesn't want Dr. Kellogg."

Aaron arrived from the shop early to have the animals fed before the storm arrived. "I'm afraid that storm will be here soon. Miriam, can you bring in extra water while I bring in more firewood? Mrs. Polinsky came by the shop to tell me the baby could arrive tonight."

"I'm afraid, Father. Mother only wants Mrs. Polinsky here to deliver the baby, but with the storm coming, you may not be able to go pick her up. That means you and I will have to deliver the baby," Miriam said almost in tears.

"That baby and Mother are in God's hands, Miriam. We will have everything prepared, and ask God to give us the wisdom to do the right thing when the time comes. I remember that we thought you were going to arrive any minute, but a whole week went by before you actually arrived," Aaron commented.

"Supper is ready. The girls are in talking to Mother. They don't like to have her where they can't see her. They think she is sick, but Anna is keeping them quiet by reading stories so they won't disturb her too much."

Sitting around the supper table that night, Aaron said, "Girls, your baby brother or sister may arrive tonight. I want you to be extra good and go to bed early so we can all be rested. Can each one of you pray for our new baby, and that God will protect us all in this coming storm? Do you want to start, Anna?"

They each prayed, even little Emma who said, "Jesus, help Mommy and my baby. I want a little brobber. Amen."

Miriam looked out the window as she and her father were preparing for bed, "Look, Papa, it is snowing heavily, and the wind is blowing drifts already. What are we going to do?"

"I'm going to put more wood in the stove, and we are going to bed. That baby's arrival may not let us rest for long, but we need the rest," Aaron said.

Aaron had just gotten into bed when Lydia started groaning, "Oh, Aaron, I think it is time. The pains are starting; you better go for Mrs. Polinsky."

Aaron dressed and then woke Miriam. "Your mother thinks the baby will arrive soon. I'm going for Mrs. Polinsky. Start heating lots of water, and stay with your mother until I return."

"But Father, what if you don't get back with Mrs. Polinsky in time? I can't remember all that Mrs. Polinsky told me to do."

"God will show you. Keep praying that I can make it through the snow. Ginger is a strong horse, so if any horse can make it, she can." Dressed in his warmest clothes, Aaron stepped out into the storm.

Miriam put several kettles of water on the stove and tossed in more wood. Walking in to check on her mother, she heard groans and her mother praying, "Lord Jesus please help this baby to arrive safely, and bring back Aaron and Mrs. Polinsky soon."

Miriam walked to the bed and touched her mother. "Are you all right, Mother? Is there anything I can get you? I have the water heating," she said trying to keep back the tears.

"Miriam, where are all those supplies that Mrs. Polinsky left? Get them out, and some baby clothes from my dresser. Find some old sheets to put on the bed. You may be the first one to hold your baby brother or sister. Read over that chapter on childbirth from the book Mrs. Polinsky left us."

The wind howled around the house as Miriam sat down to read the chapter on childbirth. A sudden call from her mother startled Miriam. "Come quick, Miriam. I think this baby is coming faster than I thought. How long has your father been gone?"

"He's been gone almost twenty minutes, Mother. What can I do to help?" Miriam asked anxiously.

"Bring me a cool cloth for my head, and a sheet to put under me. Bring a bucket of hot water, a basin, and some cloths. This baby isn't going to wait for Mrs. Polinsky. Oh, oh, here comes another pain," Lydia stopped talking to wait for another contraction to pass.

"It's coming, Miriam," said Lydia groaning loudly. "Hold onto my hand while I push. Have you brought the boiled string to tie the cord?"

"It's going to be all right, Mother. I can see the baby now. It's so exciting to be the first to see my own brother or sister," Miriam exclaimed. "It's a girl, Mother. Another little sister."

Miriam was bathing her baby sister when Mrs. Polinsky came shuffling in all out of breath. "You did it, Miriam! I knew you could. Take the baby out by the stove to dress her, and I'll take care of your mother."

"Look, Papa!" she exclaimed to Aaron as he came in from the storm. "I have a new baby sister. A little one created by God. It's so wonderful. I never dreamed it could be so exciting to help a baby to be born. God did help me to stay calm. I would love to help other mothers with their babies."

"Maybe you can some day, Miriam. You have done a marvelous job taking care of your mother and new little sister. By the way, what are we going to name this little girl?" Aaron asked.

"I would like to name her Elizabeth, after the Bible lady who was John the Baptist's mother. Do you think Mother would like that name?" Miriam asked.

"As soon as Mrs. Polinsky comes out, I will talk to your mother and we will see if she likes that name. Sounds good to me. Since you helped to bring her into the world, you should have first choice on her name," Aaron smiled graciously.

Miriam took the little red bundle, dressed her in a nightgown, and wrapped her tightly in a blanket. She snuggled her up against her shoulder and whispered into her little ear. "I love you little one. Just look at your tiny fingers gripped around my big finger. They are so perfect, each one with a finger nail. Dear Lord," she prayed, "thank You for creating little Elizabeth just the way you wanted her, and thank You for showing me how to help mother."

Mrs. Polinsky came out of the bedroom and announced, "You have all the makin's of a midwife, young lady. I could use a young lady like you to take over once I get too old to keep up with the midnight calls. Think you'd ever want to learn about delivering babies?"

"God showed me how to help Mother, I couldn't have done it on my own. But it is wonderful seeing God's creation of a new little one like Elizabeth. Maybe someday I could work with you, just maybe I could...." Miriam mused.

Lydia called weakly from the bedroom, "Isn't anyone going to bring little Elizabeth for me to see?"

"Miriam, you better take that little one to see her mommy. She will need to eat before long, and they need to get acquainted," Mrs. Polinsky said jokingly.

"Are you going to take Mrs. Polinsky home tonight, Father? Maybe she could teach me some more about delivering babies while she is here."

"Her husband said for her to stay the night. He didn't want either of us out in the storm any more tonight. It's blowing so hard that you can barely make out the road. If Ginger hadn't known the road home so well, I don't know if we would have made it. Thank God, I got her here in time," Aaron rejoiced.

"Your daughter delivered that baby, Mr. Jensen. She wouldn't have needed me. She has all the makins' of a fine midwife, if I don't miss my guess. Yes, siree," Mrs. Polinsky raved.

The next day, the snow continued to drift all morning. By afternoon, the sun came out and cutters were beginning to move past the house as businessmen tried to get to their businesses.

"I think we can safely deliver you home, Mrs. Polinsky, if you are ready to go," Aaron announced.

Aaron and Mrs. Polinsky were barely out of the yard when a cutter, pulled by two black geldings, came sliding up to the door. "Look, Miriam, here is Melody! How did she know we had a new baby? She seems all excited about something. She didn't wait for Jackson to help her down."

"Well, get the door before she breaks it down, Anna. Must be urgent for her to come now, through the deep drifts."

Miriam was holding Elizabeth when Melody burst in the house, "Where did that baby come from? I didn't know you had a new baby! When was it born? Can I see it? What is it?" she asked breathlessly.

"To answer your third question, it was born last night and it is a girl; I helped deliver her, and her name is Elizabeth. So what other questions do you have? But before you ask any more, I have a question for you. Why are you out with the roads barely opened?" Miriam asked.

"I couldn't wait to tell you that Mother told me last night that we are going to have a baby next fall. Finally, I will have a brother or sister. I was so excited, that I couldn't wait another minute to tell you. What did you say? Did I hear you say that you delivered this baby? How could you do that, you haven't been trained or anything like that?" Melody quizzed.

"God gave me wisdom. Father had gone after Mrs.

Polinsky, but the baby wouldn't wait, so I helped Mother and was holding baby Elizabeth when they arrived. God helped me stay calm. I was so scared when Father left to pick up Mrs. Polinsky — I didn't know if I could do it," Miriam reported.

"I could never do that. I have never taken care of a baby. I won't know what to do with a baby brother or sister. I probably will drop it or something. Could you teach me some things about babies?" Melody requested.

"Better than that, you can come take care of Elizabeth any time. You'll learn, Melody, you really will. I did, and I think I would like to help other mothers when I grow up. Mrs. Polinsky wants to teach me to be her helper."

"Just think, we both are learning some new lessons. Do you realize that in five years we could be married? That is sort of frightening cause I don't even know how to cook, let alone take care of a baby like you do."

"Yes, we both have done some growing up this year, Melody. We've both had to make some hard choices that we really didn't want to make, but they were right choices. God is teaching us that He can be trusted with every detail of our lives. We may have more dilemmas ahead, but God has it all planned for our good. Isn't that wonderful?" Miriam whispered gently.

— *The End* —

Coming next in the Miriam Series:
The Courtship of Miriam

AUTHOR'S
NOTES

ALTHOUGH THE STORY and the main charac-
ters in this book are fiction, there is a town of Beloit,
Kansas, today with over 4,000 residents. It is situated in
north central Kansas along the fertile valley of the
Solomon River.

From the *Mitchell County Historical Book*, the 1895
copies of the *Beloit Gazette* and *Weekly Beloit Courier*, I
learned many details of the early history of Beloit, and
found it to be a thriving town at that time, with several
newspapers, numerous doctors, several banks, quite a
number of churches, a high school, and regular entertain-
ment and speakers at the Opera House. They also had two
daily trains through all points in Kansas, Missouri, Indian
Territory and Texas, with buffet cars.

Beloit was organized as a third class city in August

1872, and by 1875 the population was 4,885, at which time it became a second class city. Timothy Hersey was the founder and first mayor. The town was first called Willow Springs, but Mr. Hersey changed it to Beloit, a French name, after Beloit, Wisconsin.

In order to secure the selection of Beloit as the county seat, Mr. Hersey personally, at the cost of $4,000, built and paid for the first court house. Before coming to Beloit, Mr. Hersey had been captured by Pawnee Indians and held for three days. The same year, Cheyennes chased him for fifteen miles and he was wounded eight times by arrows.

At Beloit, Mr. Hersey put up a saw mill and grist mill. There is a street named after him in Beloit today.

Beloit had a New York Mercantile Store in 1895, which was the year they sold out with $50,000 worth of merchandise. They had dry goods, clothing, groceries, and shoes, and they purchased live chickens, ducks, geese and eggs from their customers.

The Indian stories in this book were taken from *Pioneer Women of Kansas* by Joanna Stratton.

The *Annals of Kansas 1886-1925* told of the Kansas State Fair being held in Wichita, and William Jennings Bryant being the speaker.

A bank robbery did occur in Kansas at that time but it was in Pleasanton, Kansas, and all the details were carried in the *Beloit Weekly Courier* in March 8, 1895.

Carrie Nation did lead a raid of the Women Christian Temperance Union on open saloons in Beloit in the early 1900's. She was later arrested, but always had enough money to pay her bail. As for one saloon, it never reopened in Beloit, due to bankruptcy.

William Allen White was beginning his career as editor of the *Emporia Gazette* about that time.

The Jensen family and Cramton family are fictitious as is Reverend Stanwick. Although the ages of the Jensen family girls are similar to the ages of six girls in Beloit who inspired the writing of the story, none of the events portray any true events from their lives.

— *Donna Adee*

The Author:

This is Donna Adee's first historical novel. She has written many stories about life on their farm in central Kansas, some of which have been published in farm magazines. She has also written biographical sketches for magazines such as *Mature Living* and *Parenting Treasures*.

Her first book, *God's Special Child, Lessons from Nathan and Other Children With Special Needs* is the story of their son, Nathan, who was born with Prader Willi Syndrome. This book has been an encouragement to parents whose children have many types of special needs.

Donna and her husband, Ellis, are parents of two other children, Chris and Eric, and have four grandchildren.

The Cover Illustrator:

Ann Gower lives with her husband, Dan, and niece, Lindsey, on a farm near Tonganoxie, KS. Ann has done wild life pictures for the Denver National History Museum and pastels for the director of the Denver Zoo. Her carefully researched historical mural covers a wall in the Tongonoxie city library.

Chapter Illustrator

Tony Hoffhines lives with his wife, Ginger, and children, Jacob, Courtney, and Abby, near Tonganoxie. Tony is a graphic artist, doing brochures and advertising for corporations and stores. He has done some freelance work for the city of Tonganoxie, and portrait work for friends and family. This is his first illustrating of a book.

ORDER FORM

Please send _____ copies of *Miriam's Dilemma,* at $8.95 + $3 shipping or two or more at $9 each and we do the shipping.

If you would be interested in Donna Adee's other book: *God's Special Child — Lessons from Nathan & Other Children with Special Needs,* it is $8.95 + $3 shipping.

Both can be ordered from:

HARVEST PUBLICATIONS
1928 Oxbow Road
Minneapolis, Kansas 67467